Books by H

Sexy Snax

Streetlight People

Single Titles

Lost Time
If You Can't Stand the Heat
The Best Of Both Worlds
Rock Me Gently
Gave Good Face
Hard and Fast

Rock Me Gently

ISBN # 978-1-78651-919-1

©Copyright HK Carlton 2016

Cover Art by Posh Gosh ©Copyright 2016

Interior text design by Claire Siemaszkiewicz

Totally Bound Publishing

This is a work of fiction. All characters, places and events are from the author's imagination and should not be confused with fact. Any resemblance to persons, living or dead, events or places is purely coincidental.

All rights reserved. No part of this publication may be reproduced in any material form, whether by printing, photocopying, scanning or otherwise without the written permission of the publisher, Totally Bound Publishing.

Applications should be addressed in the first instance, in writing, to Totally Bound Publishing. Unauthorised or restricted acts in relation to this publication may result in civil proceedings and/or criminal prosecution.

The author and illustrator have asserted their respective rights under the Copyright Designs and Patents Acts 1988 (as amended) to be identified as the author of this book and illustrator of the artwork.

Published in 2016 by Totally Bound Publishing, Newland House, The Point, Weaver Road, Lincoln, LN6 3QN, United Kingdom.

No part of this book may be reproduced, scanned, or distributed in any printed or electronic form without permission. Please do not participate in or encourage piracy of copyrighted materials in violation of the authors' rights. Purchase only authorised copies.

Totally Bound Publishing is a subsidiary of Totally Entwined Group Limited.

If you purchased this book without a cover you should be aware that this book is stolen property. It was reported as "unsold and destroyed" to the publisher and neither the author nor the publisher has received any payment for this "stripped book".

Printed in Great Britain by Clays Ltd, St Ives plc

ROCK ME GENTLY

HK CARLTON

Dedication

To Jase's girl

Chapter One

Jason Westlake waited for his last parent-teacher interview of the day. Not bad for his first round of conferences as a teacher. He looked around his classroom in awe. What a different direction his life had taken in the last few years.

Six years ago he had been living the rock star lifestyle. On the road, a different girl every night, if he'd so chosen. Drugs, booze, anything for the taking. No one to say no to him. He could do, say, have, anything he wanted. Sounded like a dream for any guy. And it had been a complete blast for a while. Then one day he had looked in the mirror and he hadn't even recognized himself. All his friends had gone, either dead, in prison or in rehab. He couldn't do it anymore. He was tired. His body just couldn't take the constant abuse any longer. So he'd finished up the contractual obligations that he had to honor and then he'd quit. Cold turkey. Gone home to his parents' house in Florida, dried out and hid out for a month until his father had demanded that he go and address the press who'd been camped outside the whole time waiting for him to make some kind of formal statement or to snap just one picture of him that they could sell to the tabloids for millions.

He'd done a lot of soul searching in that month while enjoying his mom's home cooking and the way she had doted on him and supported him even when she thought he was being a dick. And he knew that he had been. But she had always been on his side. He knew she was proud of him but he also knew that she could be prouder. So, he'd thrown on a ripped T-shirt and gone outside, with his overlong hair and sunglasses, and announced to the world that he was finished with the music business and going back to school to be a teacher. It wasn't what he'd intended to say, he hadn't even consciously thought it until it was out of his mouth. He'd once toyed with the idea of being an educator. Once. In, like, fifth grade when he had a teacher that actually took him seriously and treated him like a human being instead of some dumb kid. He even felt comfortable enough to share that he wanted to play guitar and maybe even sing when he grew up.

Mr Dempster. Jason still remembered his name. The one person besides his mom who had taken the time to listen and tell him he was good. And come on, how could he trust that his mom was telling the truth when she always made it seem like he was the best at everything? Mr D reassured Jason that he could be anything he set his mind to and doing something you loved was always the best route.

That kind of lasting impression was exactly what Jason hoped to inspire in his own students.

Then, at fifteen, Jase and some buddies had put a band together. The girls had gone wild when they found out he was in a band. From that moment on he'd eaten, slept and breathed music. Against all odds, they'd actually made it.

Band members came and went. By the end, he had been the only founding member of the original five, and even then he'd thrown in the towel. Living the dream had its ups, but its downs could be killer. He'd seen it more times than he'd care to admit and realized he didn't want to die that way, without having lived. That kind of existence wasn't living in the real world. It was deceptive. It was all an illusion. He'd walked out that day to make a statement to the press as Jase West and he'd walked back into his parents' house, the same way he'd been born into it, as Jason Westlake.

"Excuse me? Oh, I'm sorry, I must have the wrong room." A lovely brunette, in a floral print dress, ducked into his classroom, bringing him out of his reverie. She glanced down at the sheet of paper in her hand.

"What room were you looking for?" he asked, smiling as

he approached her, fully intending to point the pretty lady in the right direction.

"I was looking for the history department and a Mr Westlake?"

He grinned widely. "You found him." He was pleasantly surprised that she didn't already know who he was. There had been some press. It had died down considerably but it'd still made the local papers that the one-time rock star had settled down in a suburb near his parents to teach. The principal had warned him the day he hired him that if he created any negative media that threatened the school's good name and reputation in any way, that he would have no problem firing Jason on the spot. He was forewarned and understood completely. The tabloids could be relentless and entirely false.

Her vivid green eyes widened slightly. "Oh," she breathed on a laugh. "I wasn't... Huh... Jilly didn'..."

She was flustered and he was delighted by her reaction. It had been a while since he'd had quite that effect on a woman who looked like Jill's mom. It felt good. A guy didn't attract as many screaming girls when his daily uniform was a three-piece suit and not a guitar and a cigarette. He would never have guessed that this was Jill's mom.

Jill was the quintessential all-American, girl-next-door-looking kid. Blonde hair and blue eyes. Whereas her mother had rich-looking, long, thick, wavy dark hair that he'd love to get his hands tangled in, and dramatic green eyes.

"You were expecting someone older I suspect. I know they call me Old Man Westlake. But they only do it 'cause they know I'm just a little bit vain and it bugs me. It just makes them do it all the more," he confided. "You must be Jillian's mom." He offered his hand. She placed her smaller one in his. A current of electricity shot through him. Now he was flustered. His smile slipped a little as she continued to stare up at him. He felt a small tremor run through her or maybe it was him. "Mrs Markham."

Taking a step backward, she removed her hand from his

grasp and her mouth tightened. Body Language 101 – he'd just said something wrong.

"It's Clarkson," she said, tersely. He'd seen the same look cross her daughter's face a time or two.

"Oh, I'm sorry." He wanted to smack his own forehead. Jill's parents were getting divorced – he knew that. Jill had been having a difficult time with the situation. He'd overheard her talking to her friends about it. Only recently had she begun to open up and smile again. "I knew that. I apologize again, Ms Clarkson. I should have been more prepared." God, she had him floundering.

Her face relaxed some and her mouth curved a little. "I should apologize for taking up your time, Mr Westlake. I'm sorry I'm late. I had trouble getting out of work on time. I guess we should get to it, I don't want to run long and annoy the parents who are after me."

"You are my last conference today. Actually you're my final interview this go around." He smiled and tried to return to some kind of normalcy. "It would seem I saved the best for last." She ignored his attempt to flatter and maybe make up for his earlier flub. Jason pulled out a chair for her, and after she'd folded herself gracefully into it, he dragged another alongside so that they could browse through some of Jill's work.

He took a deep breath as he reached across the desk to retrieve Jill's file. "I'm actually proud to say that I've survived my first set of mid-terms and interviews and I still want to teach. My professor at teacher's college can now eat his words."

Little lines bracketed her full lips as she laughed softly. He had to remind himself where he was and that staring at a student's mom's lovely mouth was probably not a professional thing to do and that perhaps his professor had been correct all along. 'You are on a different stage here, Mr Westlake. No one cares how charming you are or how much money you have, or how many Number Ones you've had in the charts. The parents of your students certainly will not. And neither do I. You came here to learn, not hit on every female in this lecture hall. Quit wasting my time, Mr Westlake, and get back on your tour bus.' Jason shook his head slightly as the words rang through his head.

"You're a new teacher?" she asked, assessing him, perhaps trying to guess his age. They had to be around the same, he estimated, considering her as well.

"Yes, I guess you could say that I came to my calling late."

"Well, feel blessed, Mr Westlake. Some of us never find our calling."

"It's Jason, please," he said, wanting to hear her say his name.

She looked away. Her mouth tensed again. *Whoops.*

"Lainey," she returned softly.

"Lainey, then," he said. *Yeah, Lainey, that is perfect. She looks like a Lainey.*

"So how has my daughter been in your class, Mr...?" she paused as he took a breath and prepared to correct her. "Jason," she amended.

To his surprise his stomach actually clenched at the sound of his name coming from her lips. *What the fuck?*

"Some of the other teachers are, well, rather worried about the decline in her marks," she continued.

"Actually, I think she's coming back around. I mean, I know I have only been here for a few months and some of the other teachers know her better than I do, but recently, she's begun to get back into things. She's participating in class more and handing in the majority of her assignments." He opened the file and selected her last test. "See, this was our last quiz. She got a sixty-eight. Which is up from the fifty-twos she was rockin' when we first started this adventure together."

"That's good. I'm glad to hear that. She's had a rough time."

"I'm sure you both have," he said, without thinking.

She looked down at the test, engrossed in the page.

"The other teachers tell me I'm not being hard enough

on her. That I need to push her. That submersing her in schoolwork would be the best thing for her right now. She was on the road to having her pick of any college or university of her choice and this little 'speed bump' that she is experiencing is going to obliterate any chance she had to get into the school of her choosing. She's always been an excellent student. I've never had to push her. She pushes herself. At least she used to."

"And what do you think?" He turned to view her fully, his knee almost touching hers.

"I think I understand why she just doesn't give a damn right now." She inhaled sharply at the statement, her eyes darting, as if she hadn't meant to reveal that to him. "I mean, everyone goes through difficulties in their lives and they learn how to do what they have to do, despite the hardships. This is just another learning curve, a life lesson. Something that just might help her cope with things that may be thrown her way when she's in college or university."

"I think you're right," he agreed. "And you know your daughter better than any of us. She's going to come out of this stronger. Better prepared. And so are you." Without thinking again he reached over and touched the back of her hand.

She took a deep breath and licked her lips, looking anywhere but at him. Obviously the divorce had not been her idea. She was just as wounded as her daughter. It was a shame. She was a beautiful woman. But she seemed weary.

"What else have you got?" She squinted at the desktop.

He slid the file over. "Go ahead. Have a look. As I said, she's steadily getting better marks. I was a little worried at first. I even went so far as to check on her other marks present and past. She's a very smart young lady. She's going to be fine with a little encouragement from home and from us. I don't think we need to hound her but gently nudge her back to the girl that pushes herself. We don't want to put any added pressure on her either."

Lainey flipped through the file then pushed it away. "Well,

things are looking up then."

Jason smiled. "Yeah, things are looking up." Her gaze searched his. She had the most amazing eyes. He decided he wanted to erase all the worry that he saw in them.

"Well, then, thank you for your time, Mr Westlake. It was nice to meet you," she rushed to collect her purse and stand. She was halfway across the room before he knew it, like she couldn't get away from him fast enough. Jason found himself trailing after her, scrambling for something to say to keep her just a few minutes more.

"You too, Lainey." She hesitated when he said her name, then peeked over her shoulder and gave him a small smile and a nod.

"You can call me any time. I mean, here at the school," he rushed. "If you want to check in on her progress. And I will certainly notify you if I have any concerns."

"I would appreciate that. Thank you."

It had been a long time since he'd had any connection with a woman like her. In fact, since he'd settled here, he hadn't seen or dated anyone—so focused on teaching and being a good boy that he didn't have time for it. Nor had he missed it, until now. About to ask her out for coffee, he discarded the idea—she seemed to be very skittish. The conceited ass he was, he'd like to think it was him that was affecting her but he had a hunch that she was probably this way with all men. He followed her to the door instead.

"I hope to see you again," he said, then wanted to bite his tongue as soon as it was out of his mouth.

Mumbling an obligatory "You too", she rushed down the hall. He watched her go, enjoying the sway of her hips and the way the skirt brushed the backs of her knees. She had nice legs too, right down to the slim ankles and sexy strappy shoes. Squinting, he could almost make out a tattoo on her ankle. She disappeared around the corner. Sighing Jason cleaned off his desk, then turned out the lights and headed home to an empty house. And tonight he didn't even have papers to grade to keep his mind off how big and quiet the place was. He warmed up some soup in the nuker and sat in front of the TV.

* * * *

Lainey let herself into the house and smelled the undeniable signs that Jilly was cooking. Her little girl loved to cook and Lainey was thankful for it. Especially recently, coming home so late and tired she couldn't be bothered to cook just for the two of them. Luckily Jilly didn't see it that way. She liked to cook for her mom.

"I guess I should have called ahead," Lainey said holding up the fast food bags that she'd stopped and picked up on the way home from interviews.

"Oops, or I should have texted you that I had it covered," Jilly said, coming out from behind the counter and taking the bag. She looked into it. "No problem. I'll just take this for lunch at school tomorrow," she said, cheerfully tossing the bag on the counter.

Lainey watched her daughter. Maybe Mr Westlake was right—perhaps things were looking up. Jill did seem a little more like her old self.

"So, how'd my conferences go?" she asked, stirring what smelled like soup or stew.

"Good, for the most part."

"Liar."

"Well, they are concerned, I guess, but we knew that, right?"

"Yeah. I'm getting it back together, Mom."

"I know, Jilly. I never expected anything less. You know how to handle yourself. You always have." Lainey stepped out of her shoes and sighed in relief.

"Thanks, Mama. Some parents would freak at the way I've let things slide. But not you."

"Is that a good thing, Jilly? Some of the teachers think I should be cracking the whip."

"Who? Mr O'Donnell and Miss Kelly?"

12

"Yeah, how'd you know?"

"Because they ride everyone's ass. They are classic over-achievers themselves. They don't understand a kid that just 'gets by'."

"But I got some encouraging remarks from your history teacher."

"Ahh, the beautiful Mr Westlake. And what did you think of him, Mother dear?" Jilly rounded on her mom with a big knowing smile.

"What do you mean what did I think?" Lainey asked, innocently, as if she hadn't even noticed how out of this world gorgeous the man was. Why hadn't any of *her* teachers ever looked like him? She might have stayed in school longer.

"Oh, come on, Mom. Don't tell me you've forgotten how to appreciate a good-looking man. Dad's not worth all that. You're just depriving yourself."

"Yeah, well, attractive men aren't all they're cracked up to be," she said, thinking of her ex. Thad had been beautiful too. That was the problem. Everyone found him that way, and he just ate it up.

"Mr Westlake is not like Dad. He's a nice guy."

"Your dad was a nice guy too until he got rich and famous and started to believe his own hype."

Jill's face turned to stone as it always did when they discussed her father. "Yeah, yeah, football ruined him, I know." She gave a dismissive wave of her hand.

Jill ladled some stew into a bowl and set it in front of her mother, then sat down with her own bowl.

"Mmm, this is good, Jilly," Lainey complimented while blowing on the hot broth. "You should really think about going to cooking school."

"I have actually thought about that. And if Dad gets traded to the Jets or the Giants, like he wants, I could live with him while I attend one of the culinary schools in New York."

The familiar red rage settled over Lainey at the thought

of Jill living with Thad. She hated it when she went to visit him. But she tried her best not to let it show.

Deciding to swallow her anger for once, she turned the subject back to the striking history teacher.

"So, you could have warned me that he was tall, dark and all smoldering hotness, ya know."

"Who?" Jill asked, feigning ignorance.

"Jason Westlake."

"Oh, it's Jason, is it?" Her daughter's fair brow lifted.

"Yes. It. Is," she punctuated slowly and sighed as she conjured up his smoky dark eyes and lopsided grin. He filled out a suit like no teacher she'd ever seen. And he made her feel things that she thought she'd stomped out and killed long ago. He scared her.

Jill laughed and it sounded good to hear. "I know, right? He is hot. All the girls think so. And their moms, too. And even a couple of the dads."

"I've no doubt. He's quite lovely. And he, for one, thinks you're going to be just fine too."

"I will be, Mama, don't worry. You should maybe think about getting your life back too. Don't you think? Maybe you should invite Mr Tall, Dark and Smoldering Hotness to dinner."

Lainey's gaze widened at the suggestion.

Jilly rushed on. "Or less pressure, just ask him out for coffee," she softened.

"Yeah, that's what I'll do," Lainey answered, acerbically.

"You can't blame every handsome man on earth for what Dad did to you. They're not all that way," Jilly protested.

"Yes, of course, you're right. I will get my life back. In my own time. I'm just not ready yet." Lainey turned and took her bowl to the counter, only half eaten.

Coming from behind, Jill hugged her shoulders, watching their reflections through the window. "I love you, Mama. You know that. I just hate to see you alone and so sad all the time. You deserve to be happy. We all do."

"He's your teacher, Jill, wouldn't that just be weird?"

Lainey asked, not really entertaining the idea at all.

"He won't always be my teacher. Just consider it and maybe when you're ready, you could see about making some history with the history teacher."

"History. I've never heard it called that before."

"*Mom!* I was talking coffee, what the hell are *you* thinking about?"

"Coffee, obviously."

Jill laughed and left the room.

But thoughts of Jason didn't make her think of coffee. The images he conjured were of rumpled sheets and soft skin sliding over rougher skin. She shook her head. She'd been there, done that, and come out of it raw and bitter. No, Jason Westlake was not a man to mess with.

Chapter Two

Two days later, Jason stood behind Lainey at the coffee shop, just a block from the school. It wasn't a coincidence.

"Hello, Ms Clarkson," he said, from behind her shoulder.

Turning, she looked up at him and her awesome eyes showed pleasure for a brief second before the wariness returned. "Hello, Mr Westlake. How are you?"

"Fine thanks, and you?" he returned.

"I'm well, thank you," she answered, politely. "I've never seen you in here before."

"One of my colleagues told me about the place. I thought I'd check it out some morning when I wasn't running late." It was a complete lie. He'd accidentally overheard Jill tell her girlfriends that her mother stopped at this coffee shop every morning. He remembered grinning like a Cheshire cat as the idea of 'running into her' developed in his mind. Of course, that only led to a full-fledged fantasy of her inviting him home and doing exquisite things to him with those full lips of hers. Unable to keep his mind off her since he'd met her, discovering any reason to see her was a bonus.

"That must have been Mr Valentine," she smiled.

"Yes, how did you know?" he fibbed seamlessly.

"He's in here all the time," she said, taking another step forward as the line progressed.

Jason stared up at the menu board as he noted several of the other women in the shop had spotted him and were now pointing. He gave them a smile and a quick nod. For the most part, if he acknowledged people, they nine times out of ten would leave it at that and not make a big deal or ask for an autograph. Sometimes they just wanted confirmation that he was in fact who they thought he was. People often asked, *Do you know who you are*? Most times a *Hey, how are you?* delivered cordially was enough.

"So what do you recommend, Lainey?" He inserted her first name casually.

"Uh, I usually just have coffee. The cinnamon buns are good. Jilly loves them." She glanced at his expensive suit and grinned prettily. "Although they are awfully sticky, maybe not something that you should try today."

When it was Lainey's turn at the counter, Jason stood beside her instead of behind as if they were together.

"What'll ya have?" the harassed-looking middle-aged woman barked.

"Large coffee, double double."

"I know what you want," she snapped at Lainey.

"G'morning to you too," Lainey mumbled.

"Him," the woman snapped looking up at Jason. "Wha'd'ya want?"

"I'll have the same. And two croissants," he added, pulling his wallet from his back pocket.

The clerk tossed the bag of pastries onto the counter and snarled a total.

Jason handed her the cash before Lainey could do anything.

Lainey picked up both cups, along with the little bag, and wandered out of the line while he collected his change.

As he joined her he smiled down at her while she handed him a cup and the bag.

"Thank you," she held up the hot drink in salute. "I'll return the favor next time," she promised.

"No problem. You're welcome. Do you have time to sit?"

Her smile faltered. "Uh," she looked at her watch. "Um, yeah, I guess I have a few minutes."

Jason smiled widely. "Great." He ushered her to a window booth. "I only have about ten minutes myself. They kinda frown on it when the teacher's late.

"Mmm, I can imagine," she said, sliding into the seat

across from him.

Undoing the button holding his suit coat closed, he made sure that his tie didn't drape across the sticky table as he bent to sit.

Lainey pulled the tab on her coffee and took a tentative sip. Her hand shook slightly he noticed. Was he making her nervous? He hoped so.

He fought with the tab on the cup. "I hate these things. I always end up with a great gaping hole."

"Here, let me," she offered, reaching over, pulling the flap back a little more. She then slid the tongue and groove part together and it stuck.

"Ahh, an expert." He smiled across the table at her. "Thank you." He lifted the cup and took a big gulp. It burned his mouth, but he swallowed anyway trying not to cough and sputter like a complete idiot. Inwardly he rolled his eyes at himself. Where had his confidence gone? He used to perform in front of thousands every night, and he'd never been nervous or awkward. Although, fifty percent of the time, he'd either had a few drinks or taken whatever drug was making the rounds back stage at the time, before he went on.

Lainey smiled as if she knew that he'd just scalded the inside of his mouth, then looked over his shoulder.

"Do you know those ladies?" she asked, watching behind his back.

Glancing over his shoulder, he smiled and gave a half-hearted wave to the table behind them. He still found it strange how middle-aged women could sound like teenage girls in an instant when a celebrity was around.

"Moms. From school. PTA. That kind of thing. A couple of their daughters are in Jill's history class."

She didn't look like she believed him but nodded politely at his lie. "The interviews went well then?" she joked, with an all-knowing womanly smile.

"Yeah, you could say that," he answered, clearing his throat.

"Looks like you have your own little fan club. Are you single, by chance, Mr Westlake?" She continued to grin and he found he liked it very much.

"Yeah."

"Not for long, I'd say." She raised a perfect dark eyebrow.

"No. Something else the school frowns on, I'm sure, fraternizing with the parents. Probably not a good idea."

"Nope. Probably not a good idea."

Well, shit, he thought. He'd just given her the idea that it was against his policy and that he wouldn't go out with any of the moms. He definitely wanted to see more of Jill's mom. And in his imagination he already had. His eyes lingered on the tight bodice of the form-fitting dress she had on today. Her ample breasts pushed up nicely, giving a pleasant swell over the modestly plunging U shape — a nice hint of cleavage that he wanted to slide a finger into. Or even better, his tongue. He felt his cock tug at the thought and removed his gaze from the distracting curves.

Lainey watched him, her cheeks rosy, as if she knew exactly what he was thinking. But her eyes were full of warning.

With a shift in his seat he tried to take the pressure off his groin. He took another sip of the hot coffee, thankful this time for the burn.

"Want to share my croissants?"

"What?" she stammered.

He chuckled in spite of himself. Yeah, she knew exactly what was in his dirty thoughts. "I bought two croissants. Want one?" he asked again, tearing off one pointed flaky end. Keeping his gaze on hers he slowly opened his mouth and tucked the crusty morsel between his lips.

She watched him carefully even licking her lips at the same time he did, then glimpsed over his shoulder again.

"Mmm, they're really good. Have some."

"No, thank you, I should get going. I have to get to work," she rushed her words.

Fuck! He'd blown it. Again. When had he turned into such a flop with the ladies? Well, not all the ladies. He could still hear the women behind him carrying on. When had he turned into such a flop with this lady? *Uh, from the first meeting, ya dolt.* What was it about her that turned him into a gawky twelve-year-old again?

He touched her arm. "Wait." She looked down at his hand and he removed it slowly. "Where do you work?"

"I own the boutique across the street."

What an idiot. He'd been staring right at the sign across the boulevard as they sat there. It finally registered in his horny little brain—so focused on the lovely woman across from him that it hadn't twigged. "*Jillian's*. I should have guessed."

"Why would you?" She frowned and the action produced a delightful little crease before it disappeared.

"Well, I just... I don't know." He gave up trying. "So what do you sell, women's clothing?" She was dressed nicely as she had been the other day.

"Yes, clothing, jewelry, shoes, bags, that kind of thing."

"Nice."

"Well, it was nice to see you again, Mr Westlake, Jason," she amended, when he opened his mouth to correct her. He smiled, and her eyes went to his mouth. "I need to go open the store."

"Yeah, I have to get a move on myself. It was great to see you too...Lainey. I hope I run into you another time. Maybe tomorrow." *Hopefully.*

Giving a non-committal shrug, she peered over his shoulder again, then narrowed her gaze at the table of women. "Yeah, maybe."

Being a gentleman, he followed her to the door and opened it for her.

"Thanks. And thanks for the coffee again," she said, as the door swung shut. The sun shone off her hair giving it a rich hue of highlights. God, she was just a gorgeous lady.

"No problem," he repeated, wishing he didn't have to

run.

"Well, have a good day," she said, preparing to cross the street.

"Yeah, you too. Have a good day," he said lamely.

Politely, she gave him a tight smile as she crossed.

* * * *

"Jill! Jill!" Tammy ran into the homeroom, breathless.

"What!" Jill asked, just as dramatically.

"You'll never guess what I just saw."

"What?"

"No, guess."

"Uh, you saw Patricia Douglas with Trent Matthews."

"No, guess again. And eeww by the way." Her friend's eyes widened in mock disgust at the thought of Tammy's beloved-from-afar Trent the school Quarterback and the head cheerleader.

"Umm. You saw on the newest tabloid that George Clooney just broke up with his latest model girlfriend of the month."

"Well that's just a given and not even a guess."

"Just tell me already."

"My mom had to stop for coffee on the way to drop me off at school and we saw Mr Westlake at the coffee shop with a woman."

"Yeah, and? It was only a matter of time before someone jumped on that," Jill remarked, opening her pencil case.

"Don't you want to know who the woman was?"

"Do I know her?"

"Uh, yeah, better than anyone."

Jill's brow furrowed.

"We saw him with your *mom!*" Tammy gushed.

Jill laughed out loud. "*My* mom. Right, good one."

"No seriously. It was your mom."

For a moment Jill froze. A weird sort of coldness ripped across her shoulders.

"You must have just seen them talking at the coffee shop. They met the other day when my mom went to parent-teacher interviews. And you know my mom stops there every morning before she opens the shop. She was just probably exchanging pleasantries with the man. She's anything if not the most polite woman ever born," Jill excused.

"They weren't just standing in line chatting it up, Jill. They were sitting together at a corner table, having coffee and he was eating a croissant."

"Having coffee?" Jill asked. It was just what she'd suggested to her mother the other day. Never dreaming that she'd actually ask the man out for coffee. And even though it had been Jill's idea, she now felt funny about suggesting it. She couldn't picture her mom in another relationship, especially if it turned out badly again. She wasn't sure that her mother would survive it a second time, not even for her. And she knew in her heart that in the darkest days just after her mom and dad broke up and the extent of her father's sexual escapades came out, that her mother only made it through because she knew that Jill needed her.

"Yeah, I know right! Can you imagine, if they got married, waking up to that every day? Fuck me!" Tammy slid down in her seat.

"Married? Oh, come on. My mother will never get married again. My father has ruined her for ever having a decent trusting relationship again."

"Yeah, I thought it was weird too. Your mom has kind of sworn off and pissed off the press. I didn't think she'd pick up with a celebrity again and just invite them to fuck with her some more."

"My dad wasn't always... Never mind. But I don't think my mom knows who Mr Westlake used to be or she'd steer clear of him for sure." It's why she hadn't mentioned Westlake's fame or past to her mother. Lainey would hate him on the spot and never give Old Man Westlake a chance.

"How could she not know who he is? They are like the

same age. She would have seen or heard of him. It's not like she's lived under a rock."

"Well, maybe not. My mom's kind of a country fan, not rock or pop. The only popular music she likes is the stuff I listen to and that's forced on her. And she didn't notice other guys other than my dad. She thought he was everything."

"Jill, Westlake was on every magazine cover for five years straight."

"Yeah, but so were my mom and dad and my mom went out of her way not to look at those horrible magazines. They make up the most awful shit. And they manufacture half of it just to put people in situations that they wouldn't normally be in, then take pictures that make it seem like things are going on that aren't."

"Yeah, I know. But in your dad's case, they really were."

Jill bit her lip. "Maybe not in the beginning."

Tammy studied her skeptically. "Yeah. Right."

"Did anyone else see my mom and Westlake together?"

Tammy shrugged. "I don't know."

"Omigawd, Omigawd!" Lisa ran into class. "*Jill!* Why didn't you tell me that your mom was gettin' it on with Jase West?"

Jill covered her eyes as the image of Jason Westlake's alter ego Jase West infiltrated her mind. She couldn't picture that ratty creature with her mom. But she could see her lovely mommy with Jason Westlake. She slid down in her own chair.

"The coffee shop?" Tammy asked Lisa excitedly.

"Mm-hmm."

"They were just having coffee," Jill defended.

"Yeah. Okay. Who meets for coffee in the morning unless they've spent the night between the sheets?" Lisa said, pulling her books out of her backpack.

"I can assure you, my mother was at home, in bed, *alone* last night."

"How do you know? He could sneak in after you've gone to bed."

"*Oh,* my God! Can you imagine sneaking around with that?" Tammy fanned herself.

"Can you imagine how awkward it'd be to run into him in the kitchen in his boxers?" Lisa said.

"Awkward? I think I'd fight my mother for him," Tammy announced just as the man in question walked into the room, sending Lisa and Tammy into embarrassing giggles. "And if this is really gonna happen, you're hosting sleep-overs every fucking weekend."

Jill shook her head and slunk down farther into her seat and flipped open her binder.

Mr Westlake placed the irrefutable coffee cup on his desk along with a paper bag from the coffee shop and his briefcase.

"Hey, what's in the bag Mr W?" Boyd, one of the boys from the football team asked.

"Croissant, Boyd — my breakfast."

"Can I have it?"

"I just said it was my breakfast." Mr Westlake observed the kid, as he shucked off his sport coat, eliciting a long sigh from Tammy as his muscles flexed under the mauve-colored cotton.

"Who could get away with wearing that color and still look so hot?" Lisa said in awe.

"*Duh!* Jason Westlake!" Tammy chimed in.

Boyd walked right up to the desk and picked the bag up and peeked inside. He took the pastry out, stuffed half of it in his mouth, taking a huge bite, then slid it back in the sack. "Huh, looks like someone bit it, Mr W. Can I have it now?"

Mr Westlake gave the teenager a look of bemused tolerance. "Fill your boots, kid."

"Thank you, sir, I will." Boyd gave him a mock salute, then walked back to his seat.

"Good morning, everyone!" Mr Westlake addressed the class before his gaze landed on Jill, who contemplated the front of the room through her fingers.

"Good morning, Mr Westlake," the class sing-songed in unison.

Tammy threw up her hand. "*Oh!* Mr Westlake?"

"Yes, Miss Tremblanc?"

"Did you stop for coffee this morning?"

Jill groaned.

"Um, it would appear as though I did, Tammy," he said, motioning toward the coffee cup.

"Were you running late perhaps?" Lisa asked.

"Oh God!" Jill looked up at the ceiling and rubbed her forehead.

"No, as a matter of fact I was early so I actually had time to stop for a change."

"Early, huh? Like maybe you had a *really* good night last night and you were happy to roll out of bed?" Lisa continued Tammy's line of questioning.

"What's with all the questions, ladies?"

"Nothing, sir, just trying to figure out the new bounce in your step. You seem awfully chipper this morning."

Tammy snorted, covering her mouth as Lisa continued to stare at him innocently.

"It's Friday, isn't that explanation enough?" he said slowly.

"Yes, a nice long weekend ahead to lay around…in bed and…sleep." Lisa giggled. "I can see why that would excite a guy."

* * * *

Jason watched the girls and wondered at their odd behavior. "Open your textbooks to page sixty-three. Now, yesterday we began to discuss the influence of British customs and how they have shaped our own," he spoke as he walked to the door and closed it, quieting the noise and distraction from the hallway so that he could teach the class. Fridays were difficult enough to keep people focused. He paused at Jill's desk, noticing that she was still slumped in the seat, looking at her textbook, her hand cupping over her forehead, shielding her eyes.

Pausing, he tapped his knuckles on her desk. "You okay, Jill?" he asked, with true concern.

"Fine," she said in a clipped tone, dropping her fingers back over her eyes.

By now, he'd learned enough about teenage girls not to pursue that line of questioning any further. He continued on but not before he had heard one of the other girls say, "Ahhh, real *fatherly* concern, Jill, how sweet."

"Fuck you both!" she snapped.

Jason would have reprimanded her any other time for the language in his classroom, but for one he'd never heard her use that kind of language before, so he knew that she meant business, and for two her friends must have deserved it because it shut them up and made it easier for him to continue his lecture. But he was sure that somebody had seen Lainey and him at the coffee shop this morning — either Lisa or Tammy — and they'd been teasing Jill about it. Well, better she get used to it, because if he had his way, Jill and Lainey would be seeing a lot of him in the near future. But it put a little kink in his plan to grill Jill for more information about her mom and more specifically if she had any plans for the weekend.

Jason persevered with the lesson with only half his mind on what he was saying. More than once, he realized the students were laughing not with him, but at him.

"Hey, Mr Dub?" Finally one of the guys in the back piped up. "Is your mind someplace else today?" Henry asked.

"Yeah, like on a specific someone, maybe?" Lisa chimed in.

Jill sighed and dropped her head onto the desk.

"Why do you ask?" Jason asked.

"Well, let's see. Maybe the fact that you just read the same paragraph four times, and stumbled over the same word all four times."

"I did? Why would you let me repeat the same passage

that many times and not tell me?"

"Because it was freakin' hilarious and you are wasting our time," Henry explained.

Jason mentally gave himself a kick. He needed to shake himself out of this Lainey fog. It was quite ridiculous. He'd had women crawling all over him, sometimes more than one at a time and once or twice too many to handle at once. But that was also in a fog, a drug induced one. So what was it about this little woman that had so captured his attention? She wasn't even his usual type. "What did I say?"

"It says 'to best the British'..." Tammy supplied.

"And you kept saying..." someone else spoke up.

"To breast the British," the whole class, except for Jill, sing-songed his gaffe, in unison.

He actually felt himself blush. Him. Blushing. The group erupted in uncontrollable laughter.

Jason dug his thumbs into his eyes but couldn't help but appreciate the humor in the situation. Yeah, he was obsessed with her breasts. He could still see, behind his closed lids, the plump fullness thrusting nicely out of her dress. Laughing too, he smoothed his hand from his eyes and down over his face, stopping to cover his mouth. But it wasn't just her stunning attributes that had piqued his interest.

"Okay, ya caught me. Not that it is any of your business but since I'm sure you are all mature enough to appreciate and may have even been in this type of situation before, where you can't keep your mind on task because of a girl or a guy," he encompassed the ladies in the class as well. Jill's eyes were huge and she sat up straight in her chair for the first time. "But yeah, I think I've met someone that makes me forget what I'm doing sometimes."

"At the coffee shop perhaps?"

Feigning ignorance, he gave a little shake of his head. "The coffee shop?"

"Yeah, did you meet her at the coffee shop?" Lisa asked.

"No, I didn't meet her at the coffee shop." He noticed Lisa's and Tammy's faces drop with that announcement. He didn't dare look at Jill for her reaction. But he heard whispered condolences from her friends. At least that little tidbit had gotten the desired effect. They now thought he was involved with someone other than Lainey and they would keep off Jill's case about it.

"I've never been to that particular café before. One of the other teachers suggested it." He decided to stick with that particular lie. "What is everyone's deal with the coffee shop today? I stopped for a cup, what's the big problem? I won't do it again, if it's such a serious issue, people."

"Now don't be hasty, Dubya," Boyd crooned. "I personally would enjoy a croissant every morning."

"Not gonna happen, Mr Tanner," Jason retorted. "You can have breakfast at home from now on, 'cause I'm starving." He placed a hand over his stomach for effect.

"So where'd ya meet her?" Tammy asked.

"Again not that it's any of your business, but I met her here at school." It was not a lie. He'd met Lainey here.

"Oh, is she on staff?" someone else asked.

"Maayyybee," he drawled. "But that's all you're gonna get from me, so let's get back to work and I apologize for my lapse and lack of professionalism." He hazarded a look at Jill. She squinted at him with a combination of suspicion and maybe even hurt. Perhaps she didn't want him to date her mother but she now wondered what he thought was wrong with her mother that he didn't want to date her. He couldn't win here. He skipped over her as if he had no idea what she was thinking. Although he wondered if it would all blow up in his face if Jill actually believed his little lie and told her mother that he was interested in someone here at school. But he also knew how smart Jill was and if she thought about it, she'd realize that he'd met her mother at school, during the interview. All the subterfuge was giving him a headache.

"Henry, since you were so kind as to call attention to my

lack thereof, you may continue reading, please."

"Ahh, frig," he bellyached but did as he was asked. They passed the rest of the class without any more ribbing, but he sure heard it all as they trooped out after the bell rang.

Jason made it through second period without incident. At least he thought so—he couldn't actually keep his mind on anything. And at lunchtime he did something he'd never done before. He withdrew a student's personal file for information about something other than the student. After pulling Jill's file he went back to his classroom to leaf through it and eat his lunch.

"Mother's name Lainey Clarkson." His stomach twisted in that crazy way it did when you had new-found feelings for someone. He already knew that she'd gone back to her maiden name. He wondered how long it had been dragging on. She still seemed quite raw over the whole thing and so did Jill at times. "Occupation store owner. Father Thad Markham." Something pulled at Jason's memory. "Thad Markham," he repeated. "Why does that name seem familiar to me?" He pulled out his laptop and flipped it open, Googling 'Thad Markham'.

"Wide receiver for the Jaguars. Huh, impressive, I guess, if you like the athletic type," he said aloud.

"Wow, Teach, you are seriously losin' it." Henry walked into the classroom. "Now you're talking to yourself. This woman you met must make Megan Fox look like my Mrs Hightower."

"Mrs Hightower?"

"The lunch lady." He indicated her short stature with his hand. "Looks like a troll." He shuddered dramatically.

Jason laughed. God he loved these kids. It was times like this that he knew that he'd made the right decision to become a teacher. "You shouldn't say things like that, Henry."

"I know but let's face it, you and I were both at the head of the line in heaven when the looks were handed out. Seriously, I think we went back for seconds."

"...ow, but you missed the modesty line, son."

"What does that mean?"

"Look it up. What are you doing back here?"

"I forgot my binder." He sauntered to the back of the class and retrieved it. "Hey, Dubya," Henry said, coming back up the aisle. "I've been scoping out the ladies in the office, the female teachers, even the student teachers and EAs. Seriously, dude, I think you were yankin' us. There are no babes in this school."

"I didn't actually say she was on staff."

"Ya kinda led us to believe that."

"I said I met her here at school. Lots of people come and go in this place."

"Come and go, nice choice of words there, Teach. The way you were mooning over her breasts this morning leads me to believe you haven't exactly hit it yet."

"Enough, Henry. My love life or lack thereof is not public domain anymore."

"Yeah, you sure did alotta chicks over the years."

Jason crossed his arms and gave Henry his best censorial frown.

"You've mastered that one, Dub. I'm reasonably chastised."

When Jason gave him another glare, Henry laughed and said in his wise-ass way, "Look it up."

"You are smarter than you let on, Henry."

"Yeah, well, ya know sometimes the ladies dig it when you use big words. See ya, Dub."

"Have a good weekend, Henry," he returned, on a chuckle.

"You too, Romeo."

"Smart ass."

Henry snorted. "Hey, Teach? Did I hear you say Markham when I first came in?"

Jason wasn't sure how to handle this one. He had said it, but he didn't want Henry telling Jill that he'd had her file.

"Is something wrong with Jill? Like you're not gonna call

her Dad, are ya? I mean, I *know* she and her mom have been through it since that fuckin' bastard did what he did, but—sorry for swearin' in your class, man—but seriously, he's an asshole. Don't call him, that's the last thing they need. If Jill needs tutoring or something, I'd be more than happy to help her out or find someone who can. She's just getting back to being like she used to be—don't bring him here to fuck with them, or give him any more ammunition."

Wow. Jason had never seen Henry so serious about anything.

"What do you mean, Henry? What'd this guy do to them?"

"What, do you only read your own bad press?"

"No, I don't read that crap at all. I try not to even notice those rags when I'm in a store. It was awesome when I first started out—any publicity was good publicity—but then it just got to be a damn nuisance. They build ya up just to tear you down."

"Jill's dad, he plays for the Jaguars."

"Yeah, I got that."

"He fucked around on Jill's mom with anything that moved and not just like you did in your heyday, and at least you were never married or anything. And then when it all came out in the fuckin' papers the press dragged them all through the mud. Even Mrs Markham, er, well, I guess Jill says she goes by Clarkson again." The boy shrugged. "But they crucified her and made him look like a goddamn hero. Even now, he's selling their house out from under them, he's trying to say that the boutique was totally funded by him and that Jill's mom has no right to it, and I'm not sure about the custody thing anymore, but at one time, he was trying to take Jill away."

The anger on his young face gave Jason the impression that Henry was invested in the situation somehow.

"But I think Jill's old enough to make her own decisions and she wanted to stay here and she told the judge that," Henry surmised.

The bastard wanted to leave Lainey with nothing, nowhere to live, no job or livelihood, no daughter.

"The media hounding them got so bad that at one point there was actually a cop staying with them. Overnight and everything just to keep the press away." Henry leaned against the desk.

"But then Markham accused his wife of sleeping with the guy. So, Jill's mom made the officer leave and when that didn't get that fucker Markham the results he wanted, he accused the cop of messin' with Jill when Lainey wasn't home. Jill wouldn't go along with her father's slander, but that didn't keep the cop from losing his job. His reputation was already fucked – the department really had no choice but to let him go. The damage was already done. Once those kinds of accusations are out there, people always have doubt." Henry threw his hands in the air. "He had to leave town. Anyway, after that, one night Markham showed up and Jill's mom went ballistic and no one seems to know what she did or said to Jill's old man but he finally stopped accusing her and things kind of settled down for a while. After, that's when he pulled this selling the house and taking the business bullshit out of his ass, like he wanted to punish her."

"How do you know all this, Henry?"

"Well, Jill and I, we were kinda, I don't know, in the early stages of maybe hooking up when this all blew up. I was walkin' around like a big goof, feeling all quivery in my gut every time I thought about her. I was sayin' stupid things like 'breast the British', just like you were this morning. It's pretty bad when a guy's blood flow can only go up to the brain or down... Well, you know. You got it bad, Teach, I can sympathize with ya. Anyway, for a while Jill kinda confided in me but then all of a sudden she pulled back and things haven't been the same since. I've tried to ask her but she just says nothing's wrong. She doesn't want to talk to me let alone keep seeing me."

Jason noted the football jersey that Henry was

wearing. "You on the team, Henry?"

"Yeah."

"Did you just recently make the team?"

"Yeah, how'd you know?"

"Do you think maybe subconsciously Jill is associating you being on the football team with her father?"

"What do you mean?

"Maybe she's afraid that you might do the same thing to her that her father did to her mother. Guys on the football team kind of have a reputation of being players and I don't mean on the turf. I'm not saying you are, Henry, I'm sure you'd never hurt Jill like that, but she might not know that. I'm sure she trusted her father too and, well, look how that turned out. She's young. You both are. She's just had reality slap her in the face. And she probably just came to grips with the fact that the guy she grew up thinking was some kinda hero isn't. Give her some time."

"Huh, I never thought of that. Ya think I should quit the team?"

"Well no, I wouldn't go do anything that drastic. Just don't give up on her. She probably needs as many friends around her right now as she can get."

Staring at the ground, Henry rubbed the back of his neck. "Ya know, I thought he was some kinda hero too. I used to think I was a somebody because I knew the guy. He, like, taught me some stuff and I really think it was why I got picked for the team this year. Now I just think he sucks, as a dad, as a human being. I even threw out my Jaguars jersey."

"I'm sorry, Henry. Sometimes finding out celebrities are just human beings can be tough."

"Look at you. All teacher-like, all mature. You grew up, why couldn't he? At least you never hurt anybody but yourself. You didn't cheat on a wife or leave your kid."

Jason shrugged. He hadn't evolved that much. Any of those things could have been Jase, but Henry was right, he'd never been married to any of the women he'd fucked around on. At the time, he hadn't considered it cheating.

"I better get goin', I'm not going to have enough time to eat lunch," Henry said heading toward the door again. "Thanks, Mr Westlake."

"No problem, Henry. Whenever you need to talk, I'm here."

He nodded.

"Hey, you know what? *You* should meet Jill's Mom. You'd be perfect for her. And she's freakin' hot, man, for a mom. I mean, all the guys think so."

Jason smiled. "I've met her, Henry."

"You have?"

"Parent-teacher interviews."

"Right. Well, then you know. Hot, right?"

"Well, I'm not sure that I'm supposed to think a student's mom is hot..."

"Why not? You're a teacher, not a robot."

Jason lifted his shoulder again.

"Well, keep it in mind. If this babe you're workin' on doesn't pan out, that is."

"Yeah, I'll keep her in mind."

"Have a good weekend, Mr Westlake."

"Thanks. You too, Henry."

Sighing, Jason turned back to his laptop and examined the picture of Thad Markham. He was a good-looking guy. He could see what had attracted Lainey to him in the first place. Jason flipped through some of the articles, reading the captions and gossip.

"Geez, what a sleaze ball." There were tabloid pictures of him doing anything and everything with all kinds of women, except his wife. Alongside they'd thrown in pictures of Lainey crying or shooing the press away from her front lawn. They called her a gold digger and a cold fish.

Jason typed in his old band name and clicked images. Similar pictures turned up on his page too. He closed his laptop and took a deep breath. If she caught wind of who he really was and that he'd led the same kind of life at one time, she wouldn't give him the time of day.

This wasn't going to be easy. Lainey and Jill had been through a lot. But he couldn't wait around and take his time. He needed to make Lainey feel even just a little of what he already was, before she found out about his past. Then it would be too late for her to just walk away. He'd prove to her that he'd changed. One small problem—Jill knew all about his past. All of his students did. The first day of school, he'd laid it all out for them before they had time to hear the rumors or look on the Internet or hear from their parents all about his sordid past.

After hurrying back to the office, he put Jill's file where it belonged.

Chapter Three

Lainey was just about to close the shop for the day when the bell on the door chimed. *Please be a paying customer.* A measly seventy dollars in sales for the day would not pay the rent again this month. But then again, if Thad got his way, there wouldn't be a shop by the end of the month.

A man stood with his back to her perusing the shelves behind the cash register. Strange, she didn't get many men in the shop outside of Valentine's Day and Christmas.

"May I help you?" As the gentleman turned to face her, her stomach flipped in pleasure. "Jason!" A slow simmer of need began deep in her belly, replacing the cold emptiness that had taken up residence since Thad's betrayal. She was wrong. Jason Westlake made her want again. He was dangerous but God did he look good in a suit. "What a surprise."

"Hi, I uh," he shrugged. "I was just over at the coffee shop and I saw the lights were still on over here and I guess I was just being sort of nosy. I wanted to see where you worked."

Jason had lied smoothly—he was getting good at it, he thought. "This is nice. Is it just you here?" He wondered how much she would confide in him.

"Yes, for now. The economy, you know. I had to let my staff go." That could be true, he'd give her the benefit of the doubt, but thought it was more than likely she couldn't afford to pay them because of the pending lawsuit. He'd read up on that after school. But then again, he knew first-hand that most of what was on the Internet was complete and utter bullshit. The only information he believed to be true was what Henry had divulged.

"Are you almost done for the night?"

"Yes, I was just going to close up when I heard the bell."

"Well, go ahead, do what you need to do. I'll wait and walk you out."

"Oh, you don't have to do that."

Steadily, watching her, he said, "I want to." He saw the pulse in her neck quicken. He grinned in satisfaction. Yeah, she was feeling the same zing of sexual chemistry that he was. But would she allow herself to go with it or would she be too gun-shy to give him a shot?

She slid behind the counter and began to count the cash.

"Not many sales today?"

"No," she said downheartedly. "It was a slow day."

"Well, maybe tomorrow will be better."

Graciously, she smiled as she stuffed the few twenties into the overnight bank deposit bag. After closing the register, she then turned off all the lights except for the one in the display window. She retrieved her purse from underneath the counter and slung it over her shoulder.

Jason followed her out of the door. She locked it then dropped the keys into her bag.

"It almost doesn't seem worth taking to the bank, does it?" She held the green bank bag in her hand but when she looked up at him another pang of pure lust shot straight to his gut. He thrust his hands into his pockets, knowing what would happen next. The kid was right—either the brain or the cock got the blood flow, never at the same time.

"You doing that right now?"

"Yes, it's on the way to my car anyway. The bank is just down there." She pointed to the neon sign down the street. He didn't like the thought of her walking all that way alone with any amount of cash on her.

He looked up at the sky. "It's a nice night, mind if I walk with you?"

"No. Sure." As she put one sexy foot in front of the other, he dropped in beside her. "So how was *your* day?"

An unbidden image of Lainey standing in his kitchen, asking him that very same question as he came home from work, popped into his mind. He shook his head.

"It was good, I guess. It's hard to keep their attention on a Friday and it gets worse later in the day. Their minds are on parties and dances and shopping, and friends, and God knows what else. They couldn't care less what comes out of my mouth an hour before the bell rings."

"Teaching is a noble profession. I think you are a very brave man to take up the challenge as your 'calling' as you referred to it. I couldn't do it. I guess that's why I only ever had one child. I couldn't imagine having more than one at a time to see after and discipline, let alone being responsible for all those budding minds."

She may have only had one child but Jason was willing to bet money that Jill had half-brothers and sisters running around out there. It seemed like good ole Thad shared his seed all over the country. Jason berated himself. He shouldn't have been thinking like that, but he couldn't help it.

"Yeah, but you've got a good kid. Why mess with perfection?"

Laughing in a proud kind of way, she said, "She is pretty terrific, isn't she? I guess it was a good thing Jilly had history first thing this morning. She got the benefit of your instruction before she started thinking of parties and shopping and friends and such."

It was more than evident how much she loved her daughter. The kid was her world. And for the first time in his life, Jason wondered what it would be like to have a kid of his own. He shuddered.

"You okay?" She glanced over, sideways.

"Yeah... Just caught a chill there for a second."

"It is a little cool tonight," she agreed kindly.

"I'm not really sure that anybody benefited much from my morning classes today. I was a little off and they called me out on it."

"Oh? Does that happen often?"

"That I'm a little off or that they call me out?"

"Um, both I guess."

"Well, this is the first time I've read the same paragraph four times through and didn't pick up on it myself. And because it's Friday, they just let me go on and on because I was wasting their time, for a change. But no, they call me out whenever I mess up. They live for it. Breakin' in the new teacher bit by bit."

They reached the bank. She opened up the slot and slid the bag inside.

Lainey turned back and smiled up at him. "So what did you have your mind on that was so distracting on your Friday morning, Professor? Parties, friends or shopping?" She grinned, her eyes twinkling under the street lamps.

"You," he said, before he had thought better of it.

Her expression dropped. "Me?" She squeaked as if she were appalled by the very idea. She shook her head. "I don't understand."

Well, screw it. "You don't understand why a guy might not be able to get you out of his head? You're kinda beautiful, Lainey. I haven't been able to think of much else since you walked into my classroom."

"But I didn't do anything," she defended.

"No, no," he rushed. "You didn't do anything. You didn't have to. I just really liked talking to you. And I'd like to talk to you some more. I'd like to get to know you."

Blinking, she continued to stare up at him.

"Say something, Lainey, I'm putting myself out there and you're leaving me hanging."

"I don't know what to say."

"I realize you're going through a tough time with the divorce and all and dating is probably the last thing on your mind but…"

"Dating?" she blurted, clearly aghast by the notion. "You said talking."

"Okay, talking. Whatever you can handle. Whatever you

want. Talking. Walking. Coffee. You set the pace."

"Well, I don't know," Lainey said, bewildered that a guy like Jason would want to get to know her—especially right now. She was a mess. Maybe that's just what he needed, though, to spend some time with her and find out just how damaged she was. He would go running, no sprinting in the opposite direction. Especially once he got a taste of the nasty tricks her soon-to-be-ex liked to play. It would be too much for any man to have to put up with. This wouldn't last long. But for a little while it would be nice to talk to someone different—an adult. Particularly one that looked like Jason. It most definitely wouldn't be a hardship. He'd already shown her that she might actually enjoy sex again someday. Her parts were undeniably thawing with him around. Taking Jilly's advice, she blurted, "How about coffee? Like we did this morning."

He smiled and the simmer in her stomach bubbled again.

"Coffee would be great. What are you doing right now? Do you have to rush home to Jill?"

Lainey bit her lip. Did she want to jump right in? Or should she use Jill as an excuse? But as she gazed up into his dark eyes she made the decision. "No, I don't have to hurry home tonight. Jill goes to her father's every other weekend."

She felt validated when his face showed utter revulsion at the thought. Apparently he knew enough about their life and still wanted to get to know her. It's not like their dirty laundry wasn't public knowledge and town gossip. "Court ordered. I don't have a choice and neither does Jill for exactly eight more months until she turns eighteen. Then she only has to visit him when she wants to. But she'll be going off to school right around then too. And she won't be seeing either one of us much."

Jason saw the dread cross her face at the prospect of Jill going away to school.

Lainey started to walk again and he followed.

"This is my car," she said, pausing near a nondescript gray compact.

"How about we have dinner and then coffee?" he suggested, hopefully.

She hesitated, then agreed, slowly. "Where would you like to eat?"

"I'm really not familiar with the restaurants here just yet, other than the fast food ones, that is. What do you suggest?"

"Do you like Italian?"

"Of course."

"One of Jilly's favorites is just around the corner. Batallio's."

"Yeah, I've heard of that place." They fell in side by side again and strolled to the restaurant. "I've heard it mentioned in the staff room before. I think there's even a menu kicking around the table but I've never checked it out."

Jason opened the door for her when they reached the entrance and she thanked him politely. The hostess greeted them immediately. It was quiet for a Friday night crowd.

"What, no Jill tonight?" the hostess asked recognizing Lainey.

"No, I'm sorry," Lainey said.

"But you have another friend I see." She looked up at Jason. "For two then?"

"Yes please," Lainey said.

Jason was panicked as the hostess continued to stare at him. He knew he was about to be outed and his chances with Lainey would be over before they had begun.

"You look familiar. You look like that singer," the hostess stated.

"Yeah, I get that all the time." How people recognized him without all the long hair and the scruffy beard, he'd never know.

The hostess laughed. "Oh well, then I hope I didn't insult you."

Not until she'd said that. "No, of course not. He's a great-looking guy, if I do say so myself." Jason waited until

Lainey had slipped into the booth then slid in the other side so he could watch her. Another time, he'd sit right up close to her, but for tonight he wanted to learn every nuance of her face.

"Can I start you off with a drink?"

"Want some wine?" Jason offered.

"No, I'd better not, I have to drive."

"Right. We both do," he said, with disappointment. He would be going home alone tonight. *Slow, Jase,* he reminded himself. Back in the day, he would have had a whole bottle of wine and not worried about how he was getting home. Nine times out of ten someone would pour him into the bus and they'd drive all night to the next gig and he'd sleep it off. Take an upper to get on stage and a downer when he stepped off the stage and start the cycle all over again. "We'll both have coffee." The hostess left them with some menus.

"What singer does she think you resemble?" Lainey asked, scrutinizing him over the table.

"I don't know. Some lead singer in some band. I get it all the time."

"I can't think of what band you mean. I'll have to ask Jilly. She'll know."

"She might not. It's a band that broke up years ago. Kids as young as Jilly, I mean Jill wouldn't know." He hoped she didn't ask her daughter. He was certain that Jill wouldn't lie to her mother and he wouldn't want her to. "What do you recommend?"

"I really enjoy the manicotti, but Jilly loves the spaghetti with mushrooms. The chicken cacciatore is good too."

"Mmm, it all sounds good."

"It's all good. You can't go wrong here."

The waitress brought some garlic bread. "Are we ready to order?" she asked, looking from one to the other.

"I'll have the manicotti please," Lainey answered.

"I'll have the same." Jason gathered their menus and handed them to the waitress.

Her eyes rounded and so did her mouth. "Hey! Aren't you from that band? Aren't you Ja—?"

"No, that's not me," he interrupted. "We just went through this with the hostess. Not me. Pass it on."

"Sorry. But you look just like him."

"Him who?" Lainey asked.

"Don't encourage it, Lainey," Jason cautioned gently.

The waitress walked away.

"I just wanted to know. I want to Google him. I want to see for myself if you look like this guy," Lainey explained smiling, obviously enjoying his discomfort.

"Why? I'm better-looking. Period."

"And modest too."

"I'll have to tell Henry that we must have hit that line twice too."

"What?" she laughed. "Henry?" Her smile tilted a little. "How is Henry? I haven't seen him in a while. He and Jill were kinda tight there for a while."

"He's good. He made the football team."

"Ohhh. That explains it then."

So, he had been right. "Too much like her dad?"

Her gaze met his. "I'm guessing. How much do you know about my life, Mr Westlake?"

"Mmm, back to Mr Westlake. Not good. I know some but it doesn't matter to me. Everyone has a past."

"So then tell me about yours."

That was the last thing he wanted to do. Out and out lying to her was not an option. When the time came and she found out about him he didn't want her to accuse him of just that. Then she'd never trust him. He'd be no better than her dishonest cheating husband and Jase didn't want that. "I don't want to talk about me. I want to get to know you."

"Everything about my life leads back to my divorce and I don't want to think about it let alone discuss it."

"Okay, so let's talk about your hobbies. What do you like to do?"

"I like to read."

"What do you like to read?"

"Anything."

"History books perhaps?" He grinned.

"Yes. Sometimes."

"How about romance novels?" he teased.

"I haven't read one of those in a very long while."

"Maybe you should."

"Maybe *you* should," she countered.

"Maybe I will."

"Get a historical romance. That'd be right up your alley."

"Is there such a thing?" he asked, naively.

"Oh, your knowledge of romance novels is sorely lacking, Professor." She smiled and took a small sip of the water.

"I will endeavor to be more informed. What else do you like to do?"

"I like to hike, which I also haven't done in a long time."

The waitress brought their food.

"Wow, that's really quick," Jason commented.

"They don't fool around here."

"I guess not. Smells delicious," he said, inhaling the spicy aroma. He cut into it to let some of the steam out so that it would cool off. His mouth was still a little tender from the hot coffee this morning.

"So how about tomorrow?" he asked.

"Tomorrow?" she asked, passing him the Parmesan cheese after sprinkling some onto her pasta.

"Hiking. You and me. Tomorrow?"

Her face showed disappointment. "I can't. I have to work." Although he was let down that she had to work, he was encouraged by her reaction.

"How about Sunday then? Do you open on Sundays?" He took a bite of the pasta. It was incredible.

"No, I don't. But I've recently started going back to church. I grew up going every Sunday when I was a kid. Well, forced to by my father. It's different when you choose to go, somehow. And since everything that's happened, I don't know," she shrugged. "I just feel like I need something to believe in again, you know?"

"Yeah, I get that. Had an epiphany of my own once."

"Really?" She took a dainty bite.

"Yeah, the day I decided I wanted to be a teacher."

"Tell me," she pleaded her eyes shining with unconcealed interest.

"I will but not today. What time does church end?"

"About noon."

"Then you'll hike with me?"

"Sounds good. I'll pack us a lunch."

"That sounds even better."

"What do you like on a sandwich?"

"I'm easy."

"Most men are, but what do you like on a sandwich," she teased.

"I will have you know, I am cheap but not easy."

She giggled. "That looks like a very expensive suit, Professor. *You* are not cheap."

He chuckled. "This is really good, Lainey."

She thought that he was talking about the food. "I think it's the best Italian food in town."

All of a sudden a cellphone chimed making them both jump. "Oh, that must be Jilly. She must be at her dad's by now. She calls when she lands so that I don't worry. Do you mind?"

"No, of course not, get it."

"It's just a text." She sounded disappointed. She dug into her purse and pulled out her cell then slid on a pair of reading glasses. After reading the text, she seemed to wilt.

"Is everything all right?" Jason asked.

"Yes. I just wish she'd called. I like to hear her voice. I can't tell by a text how she is really feeling but I always know by the inflection in her voice. Even when what she is saying sounds good, I know when things are not. It either means her father or someone else is in the room, or she's just trying to make it sound like she's having a good time so that I'm not worried and unhappy the whole time that she's gone. Sometimes I wonder who's the parent?"

Jason reached across the table and touched the back of her hand. "You are a great mom, don't you ever doubt it."

"That's very nice of you to say, but you don't even know me."

"Maybe, but I'm getting to know you and from what I've seen you are doing a fine job. And I've known Jill longer than I've known you and she's a great kid and great kids come from good parents. You kind of get to know what kids are like seeing them every day and how they act. You know what kind of home life they have by the way they cope and by the way that they treat other people regardless of what kind of grades they pull down."

Gazing down at the screen, she sent a response.

"And you look damn sexy in those glasses, Lainey."

She blushed but laughed. "They make me look old."

"Naw-uh, you look like a naughty librarian." He grinned and raised his eyebrows repeatedly in a lascivious manner.

She took the glasses off and slid them and the cellphone back into her purse. "And you are a naughty teacher, Mr Westlake," she commented, returning his gaze.

"Why do you say that? I haven't taught you anything naughty...yet."

She looked away and she pushed her food around the plate. There was a definite tilt in her mood since she'd read Jill's text. Even though Lainey tried to hide that it wasn't bothering her, it was obvious she was worrying about her daughter being under her father's care and influence.

"Have you ever been married, Mr Westlake?" she asked, out of nowhere.

"Nope," he answered taking the last bite.

"Any children?"

"Only about the hundred and twelve that they trust me with in a day." He paused adding, "Well, that I know of anyway." He knew the minute it was out of his mouth it had been the wrong thing to say.

She shoved her plate away suddenly and searched around for the waitress.

"It was a joke, Lainey." Well, he hoped it was a joke. He hadn't exactly been the most responsible guy for the last ten years, so God only knew what he had running around out there. But no one had ever come forward to accuse him of being a deadbeat dad and, with his money and his past fame, anyone could have come forward and claimed anything just to get a payout or their own fifteen minutes of fame. And it wasn't as if he were hiding. He was easy to find.

"Yeah, I know."

"Okay, so, I'm a teacher, not a comedian."

"I'm sorry, I'm not the best company these days. I think this was a mistake. I thought that I could sit here and play nice but I'm just not up for it. I'm sorry, Jason, I'd just like to call it a night."

"No problem, another time." Although he was disappointed he signaled the waitress who'd kept an eye on them all night.

Jason threw some bills on the table for a tip and paid the bill at the counter. Holding the door open for Lainey to exit the restaurant, he stuffed the receipt into his inside coat pocket.

They began the walk back to their cars.

"Are you going to call her?" Lainey asked, looking up the street and not at him.

"Who?"

"The waitress."

"The waitress?" He frowned wondering what the hell she was talking about. It wasn't because he'd given her any attention. "Why would I call her?"

Lainey reached over and pulled the corner of the receipt out of his pocket. She held up the piece of paper and turned it over. On the back in swoopy lettering it read 'Candi', the 'i' dotted with a heart, and a cellphone number under it.

Jason's gaze met Lainey's. "I didn't even realize she'd

done that. How did you?"

"Old habits die hard, I guess. Women were forever giving my husband their phone number in new and creative ways. It didn't even matter if I was with him. Some women just have no respect. I'm sorry, I didn't mean to look or to pry into your personal business."

He knew exactly what some women were capable of and at the time he'd taken complete advantage of what was offered. "Here, you take it. I don't want to call her."

"No, you keep it. You may change your mind. She was pretty. You probably should go out with her."

Jason stopped in front of her and waited until she looked up at him. "I don't want to go out with her. Actually, I don't want to see anyone right now, but you."

"Then you're wasting your time, Mr Westlake. I'm not ready to see people, especially men that look like you. I've been there, done that. And I will never allow myself to be hurt in that way again." After stepping around him, she then continued walking.

"So, what, are you just going to date hideous-looking men?"

"I have no intention to date at all, hideous or drop-dead gorgeous."

"Ever?"

Extracting her keys from her bag, she hit the button on the key fob and it unlocked the driver's door, as they pulled level with her car. Ignoring his question, she opened it. In an attempt to keep her from getting into the car, he placed his hand on her arm.

Her weary gaze met his.

"You don't strike me as the kind of woman who could spend her life alone." He gazed down at her, crowding her, his face close to hers.

It was then that he saw the fear coupled with desire in her eyes. She wanted him too, but she was afraid to allow herself to feel. She was a passionate woman. Of that he had no doubt. There was major sexual tension going on between them, just as he'd known from the moment she'd walked into his classroom. His heart pounded rapidly.

"You don't know anything about me."

"Maybe not, but I know what I'm feeling and you can't deny that you're feeling it too."

"But I don't want to feel anything."

"Maybe not, but it's happening anyway." He leaned down, wanting to kiss her so bad—to taste her sweet lips. He wanted to steal her breath right out of her mouth, but her eyes darted around his face and her shoulders rose in a defensive shift. At the last minute he made a detour and kissed her cheek. Backing away from her, he took a step back and another, giving her room. "Have a good night, Lainey. Drive safe."

Hoping he'd made an impact, he left her standing there, walked across the street to his own car and headed home, alone.

Chapter Four

Lainey sprayed the glass of the front display case then wiped it down with a paper towel but her mind was not on the task. Jason was the only thing on her mind and every time she thought of him that little simmer bubbled low in her stomach, sometimes sending little tingles of feeling even lower. Worse, every time the bell hanging from the door jingled she looked up in anticipation hoping to see him standing there. Then she would berate herself for it. She shouldn't want to see him. She was just asking for trouble. He was an amazing man to look at. Maybe even more attractive than Thad. Viciously, she wiped that thought from her mind. There would be no comparing Thad to Jason in any way, shape or form. Lainey didn't want there to be any similarities between them. She would prefer not to think of either of them at all. But thoughts of Jason kept occupying her mind, making her yearn for and think of things she had never thought to feel and do again. She never wanted to immerse herself so deeply in another person again.

Unfortunately, or fortunately, depending on how she was thinking at any given minute, she didn't think she would see Jason today. Not that she wanted to, she told herself. She'd made it perfectly clear that she wasn't ready for anything. But every time she replayed last night in her mind, she was certain she came off sounding like a complete and total bitch.

Why had she even brought up the waitress's phone number? She should have just minded her own business. Nevertheless, she'd felt a pang of that old jealousy and had acted on it before she'd thought better of it. She had no right to feel anything. And she didn't want to—especially jealousy. She hated that feeling. That loss of control, of being betrayed. It was something she wouldn't wish on her worst enemy. Well, maybe Thad. He'd changed so much. Lainey didn't even recognize him. She hated the Thad that he'd become and only felt grief for the man that she'd fallen in love with and lost. And he'd loved her too. Back when he had been a nobody—before fame and fortune had gone to his head. And maybe even the steroids. She wasn't sure. There hadn't been any proof. But what else could she attribute the sudden change in his behavior to? She could have handled it if he'd just fallen out of love with her. Yet the man she'd known would have had the balls to come out and tell her to her face that he didn't want to be with her anymore. Lainey shook her head. She could drive herself crazy going around and around all the theories to explain the sudden and drastic changes in Thad.

After tossing the paper towel into the garbage she then tucked the glass cleaner back under the counter. No more Thad. No Jason, she vowed, but even just thinking his name sent another wave of excited little butterflies in her stomach. She gazed into the mirror.

"What, are you fifteen again?" she asked her reflection. "Nope, certainly not. You are old and washed up. That's what you are." She examined herself disdainfully. As if a man like Jason Westlake would be interested in her. A wounded divorced single mom with baggage. Lots and lots of it.

Pulling her dark hair up, she secured it with one of the pretty new tortoise shell clips that she'd just consigned to the shop. She gave her hair another twist and held it with the identical clip on the other side. She always thought she seemed a little younger when her hair was up. Silly probably, but right now it made her feel better. After selecting a pair of elegant pearl drop earrings from the display tree Lainey slid them into her ears then stepped back to admire them.

It was nearly four. Another hour, she'd close up the shop and head home to her empty house. She hated it there now and was actually looking forward to the day it finally sold and they could leave it. The thought of Thad with other women in their house made her sick to her stomach. Apparently, he'd done it everywhere else too, but knowing he would be so blatant, so bold was just another slap. "I told you to stop that. He's not worth it," she warned herself then turned her back on the mirror.

Maybe she should just give in and let Thad close the shop too. Screw it all — him, the house, the store. Perhaps just give up everything and start over somewhere else. When Jilly started college she could just move with her. She'd give Jill her freedom, of course, to have the whole college experience, but Jilly would know that her mom would still be near if and when she needed her to be. The possibility of opening a new store wherever Jilly landed wasn't out of the question. But it still burned all the same. Just as much of her hard-earned money had gone into the place as Thad's. She'd worked her ass off at many different jobs while Thad had tried to make his way to the NFL. She'd supported them all for years. The shop, the concept, the location, everything else had been her idea from the beginning. Thad had put up half of the original start-up cost, when he signed his first contract. On opening day he'd shown up to promote the place then never given it another thought after that. He didn't care about the business or the house. *"You came into this marriage with nothing, you'll leave it the same way,"* he'd said to her. That was true. But when they'd married, he didn't have anything either. And they were happy that way.

Lainey started to do the normal things she did to close up for the day. She removed some of the more expensive merchandise out of the front window, so that it wouldn't attract any would-be thieves to smash and grab, and placed the items farther toward the rear of the store or in the back. After refolding the few things that customers had rearranged, she made sure the lights and radio were off, and locked the back door. At the front of the store, she pulled out the deposit slip and bag from under the counter and totaled up the money in the till.

A little better day, she thought. Three hundred was better than seventy. But it still wouldn't cover the rent or the insurance, or the twenty or so vendors who were breathing down her neck demanding payment. Finally getting smart, she'd been giving them Thad's lawyer's name and siccing them on him. Let him explain why they weren't being paid. If this was all his, as he claimed, then Thad could damn well pay them.

For the next half hour she did nothing but watch the clock, learning long ago not to fill out the deposit slip until she'd actually locked the door. Nothing made her more pissy than to fill it out and have a customer come in and having to redo. But it would be great if she did make another sale before she closed up.

At exactly five o'clock Lainey turned the sign to 'Closed' and finished filling out the slip. Popping the cash in the bag, she then locked up and walked down the block subsequently tossing the deposit into the bank box. Back at the car she hesitated before getting in, then looked across the street at the coffee shop and decided to run over and get something for supper so that she didn't have to cook or, worse, warm up soup for one.

The place was busy. She almost turned around and left but the smell of food lured her in. She stood in line waiting her turn, when from behind her she heard, "Well, hello, Ms. Clarkson." And the butterflies in her stomach doubled and tripled.

Unable to hide the pleasure from her face, she responded, "Hello, Mr Westlake. I'm not really surprised to see you here."

"Oh, then I have become predictable. Not like me at all. And yes, I thought you'd be here before you ask. That's not true actually, I hoped that maybe you'd come here before you headed home."

"Well, that was a mouthful of an explanation. I didn't mean to accuse you of anything."

Raising his gaze to the ceiling as if searching for divine help, he chewed quickly on the gum he had in his well-shaped mouth. "Wow, that came off cool, didn't it?" He seemed a little thrown and she liked it.

"All right, Mr Westlake, let me rephrase. I'm not surprised to see you here, but I *am* glad to see you."

Now distracted, she was suddenly fascinated by his lips. God, he was an amazing-looking man.

"Really."

"Yes, I think I need to apologize for my behavior last evening."

"No need. I think maybe I came on a little too strong after telling you that you could set the pace and the rules."

Unsure of what to say, she bit her lip. She didn't want to have to define anything. "I just wanted to have coffee, Mr Westlake," she ended up saying softly.

"Well then, we are in the perfect place."

"Can I help whoever's next?" the counter attendant asked.

Lainey was so flustered by his nearness that she couldn't remember what she wanted.

"Two large, double double," Jason supplied holding up two fingers.

While the clerk filled the order, Lainey took the time to openly examine Jason. He was dressed down today, compared to the usual designer suits. Worn, broken-in jeans clung to his shapely ass and powerful-looking thighs, while his formidable torso was topped with a tight dark T-shirt. It was so faded that she couldn't decipher whether it had been black or dark blue when new. The customary carefully coiffed hair was even a mess, as if he'd been running his hand through it repeatedly. It stood up here and there, especially at the front. It made him look younger. Cute and easy-going, as if he might be easier to approach and relate to. Not that he'd been stiff or unfriendly in the suit but he was off the chart rugged-looking, especially with the thin layer of stubble dusting his cheeks.

"You okay?" he asked as she stared at him.

"Yes, I was just thinking you appear different."

He grinned. "Yeah, I don't rock the suits on the weekends if I can help it. Not my uniform of choice, let me tell you."

"I like it," she said before she had thought.

"Why thank you." He paid the clerk and picked up both coffees. "You want to have these here or..."

She gave the café a once-over. "No, I'd rather go somewhere else, not so crowded."

He cocked his head for her to follow. Outside, he passed her a coffee cup and she fell in beside him.

"How was your day?" he asked.

"Better than yesterday by two hundred and thirty dollars."

"Well, that is better," he said cautiously.

"Yeah, better." She opened her coffee cup and, remembering how he'd had such a difficult time opening his yesterday morning, she passed him her open cup and took his from him.

"Why, thank you again. How inept am I?"

"Well, you can't be good at everything, can you?"

"Why not?"

She laughed. "How was your day?"

"Long and boring. I got up this morning when my mother phoned to remind me that she and my dad were going to a friend's tomorrow night so we won't be having Sunday supper."

"Ahh, that's sweet. You still do that?"

"Yeah, ever since I moved back here, my mom insists that I be there."

"Since you moved back? Where were you before?"

"All over. I was kind of a gypsy. Have you heard from Jill today?"

Lainey didn't miss the change of subject. He didn't seem to want to discuss his past either. What did that mean? What was he trying to hide? Couldn't be anything too bad if they'd hired him as a teacher. She let it go, for now.

"Yes, the odd text here and there. The flavor of the week took her shopping at the mall. She bought some new tops. She kept sending me pictures. *Do you like this one, Mom? How 'bout this one?* She only bought the ones I liked."

"The flavor of the week?"

"Sorry, the woman Thad is shacking up with this week. She'll be gone the next time Jilly goes for a visit. But they spoil her rotten while she's there, trying to impress her and make her like them. The way to a man's heart is through his daughter. Little do they know that Thad doesn't have a heart anymore. So, what did you do after you talked to your mother?" She did a little subject swap herself.

"I had a shower, did some laundry, went for some groceries, marked some papers, looked over my lesson plan for the week and tried to keep my mind off you. That's what led me here at approximately five o'clock."

A small shot of delight ran through her. He had a way of making her feel good about herself again, that there was still something about her that made him spend time thinking about her. That maybe she was still worthy of a man like him.

They'd walked all the way to the end of the block and into the park. They followed the paths down toward the water. The wind picked up the closer they got to it, loosening small tendrils of her hair from the clips. Jason sat down on the table top of one of the picnic benches, close to the water. Lainey followed his lead and put her foot up to step onto the seat. He gave her a hand up, to steady her, and as soon as flesh met flesh, palm to palm, that same electricity shot through her arm just as it had the first day at the school. But this time she was more aware of him and he'd thawed some of the icy walls she'd erected to keep him out.

Settled next to him she noted how he'd shifted his hips so that their outer thighs were touching.

Twisting, he took his time surveying her and when she

started to feel self-conscious he said, "I like your hair up." He reached out and wound his finger around one of the pieces that had come out of her clips, running it between his fingers. "Soft," he whispered.

"I like yours up too," she smiled slightly.

He raised his eyebrows and his sexy mouth quirked. "Little messy up there on top, is it?" He ran his hand through his dark hair just as she'd guessed he might. "Yeah," he said, crinkling his nose endearingly. "I don't really care if it sees a comb on the weekends either."

She giggled.

Jason curled his finger around her hair again, reeling her in. He was going to kiss her. Lainey was surprised to find that she wanted him to. But he tricked her by kissing her cheek again. His lips lingered warmly. She closed her eyes as the heaviness in her stomach broke free and she experienced the first real arousal she'd felt in a very long time. It scared her and it thrilled her at the same time. She could almost see herself in bed with him. All bare skin and hard limbs, sliding sinuously over each other.

He pulled back and resumed an easy relaxed stance, his arms resting on his knees. She watched as he lifted his coffee cup to his lips.

"Did you tell Jill that we went to her favorite restaurant last night?"

"No. She'd kill me if she knew that I went there without her."

His lips tightened and he nodded. "Do you think she'd have a problem with you starting to see people again?"

"I don't know what she'd think. We haven't really discussed it. But I wonder if it would be a little extra awkward for her, you being her teacher."

"Would that stop you from seeing me?"

"No, you being her teacher wouldn't stop me from seeing you, if that's what I wanted. And you won't always be her teacher."

"And you won't always feel like this, Lainey. Some day

you'll let someone in."

"I think you're right. I think I'm finally beginning to believe that maybe I won't feel like this forever."

The side of his mouth curled cockily.

He leaned his shoulder into hers.

"So, maybe," she said slowly, "you could give me a call in say, oh, I don't know, January? Is that when this semester is over?"

"January!" His voice seemed to carry out over the water and echo.

"Yes, January. When you are no longer Jill's teacher," she continued to tease him. "Well, aren't you the one that said it was school policy? No fraternizing with a parent of a current student?" She tried to maintain a straight face.

"Well, I did but I didn't mean you, I was talking about the groupies…er, I mean the moms at the coffee shop."

"I can't see that the school would differentiate. I am a mom. And Jill is in your class until the end of January. Correct?"

Holding in the giggle that threatened to erupt from her chest almost killed her. He looked absolutely stricken.

"Don't you think we should wait?"

Exhaling heavily he then responded, "Well, the teacher part of me somewhat thinks it's probably the right thing to do, but the man part of me, well, let's just say, the man part is extremely impatient," he said diplomatically.

And that just put everything into perspective for her. She didn't want to just jump into something. She was gun-shy and scared. Jason Westlake could become very important to her very quickly. And what did she know about him? Absolutely nothing about his past. What if he was a player? What if he just took her to bed then took off. Would that be so bad? No, she wasn't like that. She couldn't just sleep with him. Could she? Would she be able to do that and not get personally involved? Use him for what he so freely wanted to give and not get trampled on when he decided to move on? Or even if he didn't want to move on, what if *she* didn't want a permanent relationship again? She'd never really been on her own, outside of a relationship. She'd started going out with Thad at fifteen and never really dated anyone else. Maybe she should try dating, lots of different guys, and see what was out there.

"Lainey, you're leaving me hanging again. What are you thinking so hard about?"

"A lot of things."

"Well, maybe that's your problem. You think too much," he blurted then softened. "January! January? It's more like February. Second semester doesn't actually begin until February." And by then he wouldn't have a lot of time, going through his first real set of exams. Marking then posting scores for one hundred and twelve students.

"Can you wait that long?" she asked, looking out over the water. "I mean will you wait around for me? Or will you call the waitress in the meantime?"

He sighed. He wasn't the most patient man and he didn't know where this thing with Lainey was going. But he had never felt this way about someone so quickly. There were many women he wanted to fuck on sight, sure, and Lainey was one of them. And back in the day, he had. But this was different. She was different. The last thing he wanted to do was fuck this up or scare her away, or, worse, hurt her more than she already was. But he had changed too. He felt like he was finally growing up. And miracle upon miracles, it was time.

He reached out and slowly pressed his palm to hers, then wove his fingers through hers, stacking their joined hands onto his knee.

"I'm not going to call the waitress."

"And what if you waste your time waiting and I'm never ready?" she asked softly.

"You're ready now, Lainey." He turned slightly so that he could watch her. "Maybe you're not ready up here," he tapped her temple with his free index finger, "but I can see the pulse quicken in your neck when I'm close to you." His eyes lingered just above her collarbone as her blood beat faster for him. "I can see the fear in your eyes. But I can see beyond that, and you want to be close to me. I can see by the set of your lips that you want me to kiss you."

Her lips parted at his words and the sensual haze he was creating within her. He even leaned in slightly as if he just might kiss her and the bubbling heat in her boiled over and deep down wet arousal burst free. "But I won't. When you're ready, you kiss me. And then we'll both know."

Abruptly, he turned and faced the water again. He picked up his coffee and took a long drink while still holding her hand.

Lainey didn't know what to do with herself. He'd just left *her* hanging. Damn it, she wanted him to kiss her. Wanted him to make the decision for her and take her choice away. But the coward that she was, she followed his lead and picked up her coffee, taking a sip, then pulled her thighs together trying to lessen the burning heat between her legs. She wanted much more than mere kisses.

After finishing his coffee, he threw the cup expertly into the receptacle near then he tugged on her hand and pulled her from the table. "Come on, I'll walk you back up to your car. You need to go home and have a good meal and get some sleep."

"I do?" she said stupidly.

"Yes, hiking tomorrow, did you forget?"

"No."

Aware that he was walking quickly, he practically pulled her back up the street. And she was trotting double time just to keep pace with him since he refused to let go of her hand. But he needed to get the hell away from her. He had visions of slamming her onto the picnic table, throwing up her skirt and ravishing her right there in the park.

When they reached her car he opened the door for her and she tossed her purse inside, before turning to face him.

He skimmed his hands up her arms, stopping at her shoulders. "So what time do you leave for church in the morning?"

"About ten forty-five, it's not far."

"And you get home around noon?"

"Yes," she said looking up at him.

"I'll see you then." He placed a kiss on her cheek, letting his lips linger on her soft skin. She turned her face into his, allowing her cheek to rest against his rough one.

Her warm breath, quick and shallow, bounced off his Adam's apple. "See you then," she whispered.

Chapter Five

Lainey ran out of the door right at ten forty-five Sunday morning. She hadn't slept well and had woken in a pool of her own sweat after an incredibly steamy dream about her and Jason. She couldn't remember much of the actual dream itself. Just images and feelings and the picnic table, that had ended in an explosive orgasm that woke her up and left her feeling less raw and fidgety but more empty, which she didn't think was possible. She had showered and dressed and decided to braid her hair while it was still wet since she didn't have time to do much else with it.

Lainey pulled the door closed and started down the drive toward her car when she noticed another pulled across the end of her driveway and the darkly handsome man leaning against it.

"Jason," she said smiling, perhaps even blushing, as the horny little butterflies did the cancan in her stomach. Dressed sharply, he wore dark tailored slacks, a burgundy dress shirt and a black tie, topped off with dark shades shielding his eyes. His hair was not as sculpted as he'd tamed it for school, but it wasn't as messy as it had been yesterday when she'd seen him. It was sort of spiky but not standing straight up, just kind of sweeping toward the front. He looked like a model in a new car ad, leaning casually against the expensive red and black sports car as if he hadn't a care in the world. She walked all the way to him before he moved, straightening as she reached him. He took the dark glasses from his eyes. He looked tired too. Perhaps he'd had trouble sleeping as well. "What are you doing here?"

"I thought I'd take you to church," he said simply.

Her eyes widened slightly but so did her smile. She was pleased but said, "You don't have to do that."

"I want to. Get in." He opened the door and she sat down into the luxurious creamy leather.

After folding himself into the driver's seat, he started the engine. The car roared to life. He pulled his glasses back into place. "Lead the way, mi'lady."

She gave him the simple directions then sat back. "This is a Bugatti Veyron, isn't it?"

"Yes. You know your cars," he said, watching the road.

"Thad always wanted one of these."

He nodded, not commenting.

"You must be an incredible teacher, Mr Westlake. I wasn't aware they made the kind of money it takes to own one of these."

"They don't," he answered in a clipped tone, as the car accelerated.

He seemed cool today. He never wanted to talk about himself or his past but today, he seemed even more closed. She didn't like that. It made her think he had something to hide. Something he didn't want her to know. Maybe something that might change the way things were going between them.

"Do you steal cars on the side, Mr Westlake?"

"Nope. Bought and paid for."

"By you?"

"Yep."

"Can you park this thing in the school parking lot without round the clock security?"

"I don't drive this baby to school. I only take her out on special occasions. Or when I want to go fast."

"What do you drive to school?"

"The Porsche."

"Ahh, of course. What was it you said you did for a living before you had this epiphany to become an overworked, underpaid and underappreciated teacher?"

"I didn't."

They pulled into the parking lot of the old stone church. He maneuvered expertly into a small space with only one hand on the steering wheel. Exiting, he came around to the passenger's side then opened the door for her. He offered her his hand and helped her from the low seat.

"Thank you," she said, rising, her heels bringing the top of her head up to his chin. "You must have made very good money as a gypsy," she said, looking up at him.

"Very," he answered, looking down at her, his dark glasses concealing his mood. He stood in front of her, making it impossible for her to get around him, almost pinning her between the car and his body. She could feel the heat from him. Deeply, she inhaled the clean refreshing scent of soap and the uniquely spicy scent of Jason.

The notch in his throat bobbed as he swallowed. "Your pulse is very rapid and erratic today, Lainey. What's the matter?"

"Perhaps the Bugatti is exciting, Mr Westlake."

"Funny..." He placed his thumb over the rapid beat at the base of her neck, his fingers lightly brushing across her skin causing goose bumps to race down her arm. "You didn't even know about the Bugatti yesterday and it was still doing this rat-a-tat thing. And you know what else? The minute I touched you, it triple timed."

She felt at a disadvantage not being able to see his eyes. He seemed not quite angry, but adversarial. Like he was intent on proving his point that she wanted him too and he was going to overwhelm her until she gave in to it.

"Tell me, is this a special occasion or do you just want to go fast?" she asked, referring to his earlier comment about the car.

"I'd have to say it's because I wanna go fast but the car is the only thing that's going to get me there." He scowled.

She stepped around him. So he was pissy because she wouldn't put out. On one hand it ticked her off. On the other hand it gave her a little thrill that he was going through the same agony that she was. "I hope you'll be very happy together. Thanks for the ride." She strode toward the church as she belatedly noticed how many of the worshippers had stopped to gawk. She tried to ignore the stares. They weren't really looking at her anyway. It was the Bugatti they were interested in, and some healthy speculation about the football star's downtrodden ex-wife showing up to church with the sexiest man alive, driving *that*.

The car door slammed, then the obnoxious 'dut-dut' followed as he set the alarm. "Hey." He caught up to her in a few long strides.

"You can go. You don't have to come in. I'll see you later. It was a nice try." She tried to walk faster but he caught her arm on the steps.

"Stop."

"No. You stop. I didn't ask you to bring me here and I certainly didn't ask you to accompany me in. And I especially don't want you to be here if you don't want to be. That's not what this is about. Not to me. This makes me feel better. And I'm not feeling it right now with you pressuring me. You said I could set the pace and now you're clearly angry with me. I don't need it. Go home, Mr Westlake, and grade some papers, or better yet call your waitress. Perhaps she is faster than me *and* your Bugatti."

His nostrils flared as he took another deep breath. "I haven't been in a church in a very long time. I'm not sure the walls will remain standing if I come inside."

She couldn't stand not to see his eyes anymore. Not being able to see them made her think all kinds of crazy things, especially when he was being so cryptic about his past. She pulled the shades from his eyes and pushed one of the arms into his shirt, then folded them down.

Searching his dark eyes, she noted that he seemed guarded.

"What are you afraid of? Worse men than you walk over that threshold every day and still it stands. Men that don't even deserve or want forgiveness. If you're just here to try to ingratiate yourself with me, don't. Go in there for yourself. Not for me."

Lainey walked into the church by herself. A greeter handed her a calendar showing the order of service and she made her way down the aisle and sat by herself in her usual spot. Sometimes Jilly accompanied her but sometimes she didn't want to, and Lainey didn't force her to, like her father had done to her when she was a child. It really was different when you came for yourself and not for somebody else.

Jason paced outside the doors for a moment. One of the ushers smiled and nodded at him, as if he knew what he was going through. The doors closed as the organ music began. Jason listened to the first hymn and the voices raised in unison.

"Well, God, I'm here. And I should probably thank you for lookin' out for me all those years when I was out there doing all the wrong things. I really like this girl and I'm not sayin' I'm gonna be here every Sunday, and I'm not even sure that I'm here for the right reasons. She's probably right on that score. I showed up to make points with her. I'm sure I'm not telling you anything you don't already know. You know why I'm here. So I'm just bein' straight up with you, I'm goin' in for the girl and you'll just have to forgive me… Again."

Reefing open the door, he skimmed over the heads of the rest of the congregation hunting for the woman in question. About halfway down the aisle to the far right with the hymn book in her hand, she stood alone, singing with the rest. He walked to her side. She shuffled over to make room for him and passed the left side of the song book to him. Ignoring the words, he tried to follow the music.

He hadn't sung a note in ages. It was like the minute he'd decided to go back to school he'd forgotten all about music. As if he'd turned off his creativeness. He hadn't even written a melody or jotted down lyrics. In the past, he'd kept a pad of paper and a pen by his bedside always, even when they were on the tour bus, just in case something came to him in his sleep. He used to dream lyrics and sometimes even the first few chords of a new song. A few times he'd woken up and after having written it down, he'd get his guitar and play it out and a whole chorus, sometimes even a whole song, had come to him. Some of their best stuff had come just like that. From his head to Number One in the charts. He'd even written a couple that he'd never shown anyone else. Stuff that wasn't in their genre, but he'd always thought someday he'd publish them for someone else to record. He'd never really thought about it until now, with the sunlight streaming through the stained glass windows, that maybe it had all been a gift. His talent, the way that the melodies and harmonies and lyrics had just poured from him.

As the music ended they sat and there was a reading, some announcements and another hymn. They stood and again she handed him the book. He listened to her for a moment. She had a nice voice. He liked it. He let it wash over him. She'd sound good with him, he thought. He didn't even realize that he'd started to hum until she looked up at him and gave him a smile. Again, he read the music instead of reading along with the words. He could feel the organ vibrating through his chest, making him feel things that he hadn't in a long time.

They sat again and listened to the service. The choir rose and began to sing. Jason let the music in and he realized he had missed it. How could he have let himself turn from it so completely? It had always been so much a part of him. He totally missed the sermon thinking about everything. His mind was a whirl. Where was his guitar even? Had he even brought it from his parents' house? It had to be at home. He'd given up most of his guitars. Actually just left them on the bus and walked away from them. He'd kept the one he'd played MSG with and the acoustic that he'd had for as long as he could remember. All beat to hell as it was, it was probably his most prized possession. It meant more to him than the Bugatti — all the cars, the house, the money. It reminded him of simpler times.

Lainey reached over and twined her fingers into his. "Are you all right?" she whispered leaning in so that he could hear her.

He squeezed her hand and pulled it onto his thigh. He nodded, before regarding their entwined hands. She'd reached out to him. That was something.

The offering plate came around and Lainey put five bucks on the plate then passed it to Jason, probably expecting that he'd just pass it along. But he tossed a twenty in it.

Jason reluctantly let go of her hand as they stood to sing the last hymn. It was a song that was familiar to him, he didn't even know from where. He finally allowed himself to read the lyrics and he let the words form on his lips. He took a deep breath and he sang the first words he'd sung in over six years. Softly at first, louder as his confidence in himself and the words grew.

Lainey looked up at him with surprise. She stopped singing and her mouth dropped open. The deep rich timbre of his voice went straight through her. The congregation finished the hymn, the minister boomed his benediction, and Lainey didn't remember a thing from the moment Jason had started to harmonize.

Jason took hold of Lainey's hand again as they filed out slowly, following the crowd. The minister stood at the door greeting the parishioners by name.

"Lainey. It's good to see you again."

"And you, Reverend."

"You are becoming a regular. Soon I will begin to badger you to become a member. And I see you've brought a friend this time."

Jason presented his hand. "Jase Westlake, good to meet you, Reverend. I enjoyed the sermon."

The minister wrapped both hands around Jason's and

shook his hand with enthusiasm. "Jase. It's good to meet you. Westlake? Westlake. We had some Westlakes as members at one time. What were their given names? Oh, well, anyway, I hope we'll see you again."

Jason gave him a non-committal nod, wrapping his arm around Lainey's back, coaxing her out.

"Please feel welcome to join us for coffee and fellowship."

The pressure on her back increased, propelling her forward.

As they walked out into the sunshine, Jason pulled his sunglasses from his shirt and slid them into place. Taking Lainey's hand again, he steered her toward the car, which now had a crowd of teenage boys around it.

Lainey bit her lip wondering how he might handle this—all those kids being around the one-point-seven million dollar car. The vehicle cost more than Lainey and Thad's home.

"I'm gonna own one of these someday," one of the kids boasted.

Jason pulled the key from his pocket and unarmed the alarm, making the boys jump as if they'd been caught with their hands in the cookie jar.

"Step back, boys, and let the lovely lady through." He opened the door for her and she stepped in. He closed it and walked around to his own side. The boys fired questions at him. He answered every one of them and allowed them a look inside when he opened up the driver's side. He was wonderful with them. Another reason that he must make a good teacher.

"'Kay, guys, if you'll excuse us, we need to go. But I'm sure we'll be back and if it's all right with your parents, maybe we can go for a ride."

"Naw way!" "Awesome!" "How 'bout next week?" "I'm gonna go ask my ma now!" "Me first."

Jason got in and started the car. He revved the engine a few times and watched the young faces light up, impressed with the sound.

He pulled out of the parking spot and casually drove out.

"I'd peel outta here if we weren't at church."

"I'm sure that would dissuade a couple of moms from allowing their sons a ride with you."

He chuckled. "Yeah, but they woulda thought that was so freakin' cool."

She laughed. "Yeah, they would."

Jason hit a button and the car filled with music. He sang along to Springsteen's *Born to Run*. That was more his thing. Now that he'd used his voice again, he wanted to keep using it.

"You are a man of many talents, *Jase*."

He inhaled sharply thinking she'd put two and two together and guessed who he was.

"I think you should give up your day job and take up singing. You have an incredible voice."

He relaxed, realizing he'd introduced himself to the minister as Jase.

"That's what I gave up to be a teacher."

"What?"

"I told you, I moved around a lot. I sang. In a band."

"No way, you did not."

He grinned slightly. She really had no idea. "Yeah."

"When? For how long? What made you quit? Would I have heard of you? Is that who people keep mistaking you for? It's not a mistake, they know you?"

"Whoa, wait. That's a lot to answer. I don't know if you'd have heard of us. We went by a lot of different names in the beginning." That was the truth. But as they got to be more well known, and because he was the front man and did most of the lead vocals and yeah because of his looks, people just associated the rest as his band and it just became The Jase West Band. Like when you hear Bon Jovi you automatically think Jon. Van Halen you think Eddie, not even David Lee Roth or Sammy Hagar. "And you know what made me quit. I had a, what is it women say? An 'aha' moment? I didn't want to do it anymore. I looked in the mirror one morning and I didn't even recognize myself. I needed a change. I needed to clean up and grow up."

"Okay, so what kind of music?"

"Rock."

"So you went from rock band to school of rock?"

"Yeah, I guess I did."

"Must have been some epiphany," she commented as they pulled up in front of her house.

He jumped out and ran around to get her door. Again, he stood in front of her, not allowing her room to think.

He pushed his glasses up onto his head. Placing his hands on either side of the car's roof, he trapped her. "So, I'm gonna run home, change, put the Bugatti to bed and I'll be back to pick you up. Put on your hikin' boots, baby." He kissed her cheek. Once. Twice, moving closer to the corner of her mouth. When his lips finally touched her there she turned her face into his and allowed herself to kiss the roughness of his cheek. Then she ducked under his arms and took off up the driveway. She didn't turn back but he made sure that she heard the screeching tires and the roar of the powerful engine speed down her street. Yeah, he wanted to go fast today.

Chapter Six

Lainey changed, putting on a loose-fitting, but frilly white peasant blouse and a pair of beige short shorts. Undoing the loose braid she fluffed her hair with her fingers, scrunching it then finally letting it fall loose around her shoulders in kinky waves. She reapplied some blue eyeliner and mascara, then pinched her cheeks going for the *au naturel* look instead of applying blush. She knew that her face would flush when Jason came back around anyway.

Taking the cooler from the basement she then rushed back into the kitchen and began to throw together sandwiches. When she acknowledged the fact that she was excited to be spending the day with Jason, the horny little butterflies were back with a vengeance. It had been a long time since she'd felt this way.

After rinsing some grapes she tossed them into a plastic container. Unsure if he liked mayo or mustard, she threw those both up onto the counter to take along. She made a large pitcher of lemonade and was stirring it with a long wooden spoon when she heard the knock on the door.

"Come in," she yelled pulling her blouse off each shoulder.

"Are you always so trustworthy? Any sexual deviant could walk in and take advantage of you."

"Well, I was expecting a certain pervert so I wasn't worried," she teased, admiring the tight white T-shirt hugging his chest and muscular biceps along with the snug-fitting dark shorts.

Pushing his dark glasses up onto his head, he raised his eyebrows at her. "Are you referring to me?" he asked in all innocence. He followed her to the counter.

"Oh, look at you," he breathed. She looked over her shoulder at him, as his gaze started at her ankles moving slowly up over her. He wrapped his large hands around her hips. "Sexual deviant, right here. I knew you'd have fantastic legs. And the shorts... Geez woman, how am I supposed to walk around with you all day with that amazing ass in those tiny shorts?" Removing his hands from her hips, he then started at her wrists, skimming his palms over her arms all the way to her shoulders. She inhaled sharply when she felt his lips skim her shoulder. Moving her hair, he continued over the back of her neck and onto the other shoulder. "Mmm, creamy sweet shoulders. Yeah, I'm just gonna be indecent all freakin' day." He flattened his body against her back, pushing her slightly forward so that her butt stuck out and he rubbed his erection over it, leaving her in no doubt as to what he meant. "As if I haven't been since the day I met you." Goose bumps rose all over her body and her heart pounded.

"Oh you have not," she said, straightening her back out along his chest. Awkwardly, she raised her arms reaching behind them to clasp her hands behind his neck. He wound his arms around her waist and held her to him.

"You feel good," he mumbled against her neck, then trailed his palms over her ribs. Lainey arched her back in anticipation, then thrust her chest out as he wrapped his hands around her breasts. She sighed, loving the feel of his hands on her.

"Mmm," he hummed. "Nice." He kneaded her breasts. Her nipples hardened against his palms. He plucked them with his fingers, making them even stiffer, sending delicious little waves of sensation lower. His hips took on a rhythmic thrust, grinding hard against her ass. "Do you have any idea what I want to do to you?" he breathed.

"Ohh, I *think* I do." Surprisingly, she wanted him to do them — and even more shocking — she wanted to do things to him. Sensuously, she wiggled her bum against him. He shoved her so that her chest flattened out against the counter. He grabbed her by the hips, lifting her backside level with his hard straining cock and he ground against her enthusiastically.

As he reached around and fumbled with the button of her shorts, the phone started to ring.

"Ahh, fuck me!" he cursed, pinning her.

"Church did nothing for you, did it? Let me go, I have to get that, Jason, it might be Jilly."

Reluctantly, he released her. Lainey answered breathlessly, "Hello?"

"Hey, Mama."

"Hey, baby, what's up?"

"You sound out of breath, you okay?"

"I'm fine, I was just down in the laundry room and had to run up the stairs to get the phone."

"Liar," Jason accused softly. *"Church did nothing for you,"* he mimicked.

She stuck her tongue out at him. Then pointed to the sandwiches and at the cooler, indicating that he should put them inside.

"I was hoping I'd catch you. I figured you'd be back from church by now. Did you go this morning?"

"Yes, I did go to church this morning and you'll never guess who I saw there."

Jason hesitated before placing the grapes into the cooler and looked over, surprised, she guessed, that she would tell Jill about him, possibly smoothing the way to make it easier for her to accept him being around.

"Who?"

"Mr Westlake."

"What? Really? He doesn't seem like the church-going kind."

"What does that mean? The church-going kind? He seems nice to me."

"He's nice and all, I just...I don't know." She paused. "You've been running into him a lot lately, huh? You had coffee with him and now he shows up at church?"

"I ran into him at the coffee shop, Jilly. It wasn't a planned meeting. How'd you know about that?"

"Everyone at school saw you with him and couldn't wait to tell me all about it."

"Why didn't you mention it then, if it was bothering you?"

"It wasn't, until now that he keeps popping up wherever you are."

"Would that be so bad? You suggested it yourself."

Jason's eyes widened slightly at that little statement.

"Yeah, I know. It's just weird. I've never seen you with anyone else. And he's my teacher."

"You see your dad with other people all the time. And Mr Westlake won't be your teacher forever. We talked about this."

"Yeah, I know, but it'll just be different to see you with someone else. I just never pictured you with anyone but Dad."

"I never pictured it either, Jilly." Until now.

"And who knows, he might not be around forever either."

"What does that mean?"

"Nothing. I just mean Dad changes girlfriends so often that I can't keep track."

"But I won't be like that, Jilly. You know that."

"I didn't mean you. Westlake might be just like Dad, you don't know. The way he looks, you know he's gotta be a player."

"No. You're right. I don't know."

"Everything okay there, Jilly?" Lainey asked. She didn't want to hear that right now. She had enough of her own doubts hounding her.

"Yeah, things are good, I just wanted to let you know that my flight has been delayed so Dad's 'flava du jour' is going to drive me back this afternoon."

Having Jason around was doing wonders for her, Lainey thought. It didn't even hurt for a change that Thad was with yet another woman. She didn't care. This was a good day.

"Okay. Why isn't Dad bringing you back?"

"He has a game today, Mom."

"Oh, right, duh, it's Sunday."

"Well, one good thing while you're crushing on Jayson…" She said his name as if she were teasing one of her girlfriends. "You're forgetting all about old what's-his-name."

"What *was* his name?" Lainey laughed. Forgetting felt good.

Jill giggled too. "I better go. We'll talk when I get back. I'll see you later, Mama. Love you."

"See you later, baby, I love you too. Bye."

Jason sealed the lid on the cooler. "Everything okay?"

"Yeah, Jill's flight was delayed so she's getting a ride back."

"Oh, does that mean you need to stay close to home?"

"No, we can go." Lainey saw the disappointment register on his face that they were not going to finish what he'd started. But she was going to try to get to know him before she jumped right in with both feet. "She won't be home until later. Unless you don't want to be seen riding around in my car after '*going fast*' in your Veyron."

"Who said we were taking your car?"

"Oh? What'd you bring this time? An RV?"

"Not quite," he said, picking up the cooler.

Lainey slipped on a pair of canvas shoes, then followed him out. Soon after she locked the door behind them, as he placed the cooler in the back of a black Hummer H3.

"What, gold-plated too flashy for you?" she asked.

"I will have you know just as I am easy without being cheap. I am flashy without being ostentatious."

"Or gaudy," she added, as he helped her up into the H3.

After hopping into the driver's seat, he started the engine. Lainey looked around. She'd never been in a Hummer. She noted a beat-up old guitar case in the back. "I'm beginning to think that this 'little' band you were in was a little more prolific than you are leading me to believe."

"We did all right," he answered. "So, where are we headed? You have a spot that you like to hike?"

"I like Marsh Stone Park."

"I know where that is. 'Bout, what, twenty minutes' drive?"

She nodded and sat back to watch the scenery go by.

"I was surprised that you told Jill about me."

"I just kinda wanted to feel her out, I guess."

"Does that mean you might keep me around for a while?"

"I might. She seemed to think it was kinda strange that you keep showing up where I am."

He reached over and flipped on the radio.

"The coffee shop wasn't just a coincidence," he confessed.

"It wasn't? You said Mr Valentine suggested it."

"He didn't. I overhead Jill tell her friends that you stop there every morning before you go to work. So I thought maybe I'd accidentally bump into you."

"Why?"

"I told you, because I couldn't stop thinking about you. Didn't you think about me too? Maybe just a little?"

"I thought you were very handsome," she allowed.

"That's not what I asked. I know what I look like and I know what other people think of me..."

"Humility, again," she quipped.

"So you thought I was good-looking, so what? So does seventy-five percent of the population, but is that all you thought?" She didn't think he was trying to sound conceited. He knew he was gorgeous. It was just a fact. "You didn't think anything else? Like I was a jerk? You hated my suit? You thought I was too young to be a teacher? Too old?"

"Well, that first night, after the interview, I did ask Jill why she didn't warn me that you were tall, dark and smoldering hotness. I was a little thrown. You were not what I expected. But I told you that. I tried not to think of you that night."

"Why?"

"Because you scare me."

"Why?"

"Because I've been with a very handsome man before. Look how that turned out."

"So all of mankind has to pay because your ex is a dog?"

She looked out of the window.

"I'm sorry. I shouldn't have said that." He drove for a few minutes without speaking. "So Jill told you to ask me out for coffee?"

She nodded.

"So she kind of gave you permission. Would you have?"

"I'm not sure. Probably not."

"Because you're not ready."

"Because I thought I wasn't ready. You are rapidly proving me wrong."

He grinned, this time with arrogance. "Okay. So did you think about me after we had coffee on Friday morning?"

She bit her lip. "Yes."

"And when I showed up in your shop, what then?"

"I thought you were aggressive."

"So then why did you agree to have dinner with me?"

"You are also persuasive. And it doesn't hurt that I am in the seventy-five percentile of your adoring population."

"Ditto, baby. And this morning when I kidnapped you for church?"

"That was very well done of you."

"Scored some points?"

"With me or God?"

"You."

She shook her head but said, "Yes."

Jason pulled the Hummer into the recreational area and parked then came around to her side. Jason opened the door and reached for her. Standing on the running board, she was almost as tall as him. She wound her arms around his neck and he encircled her waist.

Lainey pushed his shades up so that she could see his

eyes. His erection was already twitching and nudging its way up against her tummy. "You didn't ask what I thought about what happened right before Jill called."

His jaw tightened and he swallowed hard, then asked, "What did you think?"

"I think you must be very well-endowed, but I'm just going by feel." She grinned.

He let out a painful sounding groan. "That's it, we are getting right back in this truck."

"Naw-uh." Lainey attempted to push past him but he held her tightly.

"Well, I can't walk around like this all day." He prodded her with his hard-on.

"Then let's just throw the blanket down and we can eat and talk. We don't have to hike if you're not able." She grinned. "And maybe later we could neck."

He dove for her mouth but she turned her cheek. "I'm going to kiss you, remember? Your rules."

"Yeah, I'm a fuckin' idiot."

"It's a good thing you're not an English teacher." She smiled, stepping off the running board.

Jason retrieved the cooler from the back and followed as she led them to a fairly secluded spot in a little copse of trees. They spread out the blanket and unpacked the food.

"Are you hungry?" Lainey asked.

"Starving and not for food," he answered.

"You are a very impatient man, Mr Westlake. We've only known each other, what, five days?"

He stretched out on the blanket. "But I've wanted you since the minute I laid eyes on you so I've been waiting seventy-two hundred minutes and counting. If you think of it that way, I am a very patient man."

She smiled. "You wanted me to what?" she flirted.

"Do you really want me to answer that? Because I'm very good with detail and I can be quite explicit and raunchy."

"Mmm, maybe later. But that reminds me. I brought you something." She stretched to reach for her purse and felt his hand slide up her thigh to cup her bottom.

She gave him a mock look of severity.

"What? I like what you brought me."

"Not that, huh. This."

"A book," he said, less than enthusiastically.

"Not just any book. Historical romance."

"Oh?" he replied, in the same tone.

"I could read you all the dirty parts."

"Although at any other time that would be titillating, I honestly couldn't take sexy words coming from those lips right now. Not unless I was buried between those beautiful thighs while you read."

"As if I could concentrate enough to read if you were."

"Are you finished teasing me?"

"Probably not."

"I'm seriously going to die today."

"Regardless of what they tell you, you can't actually die from that. Besides, once we do that, we can't go back. It's not like there will ever be that mystery again. Isn't it exciting all this anticipation?"

"No, anticipation is just downright painful. Wait a minute." He sat up straighter. "You said once we do that. Not if."

Choosing to ignore that, she said, "Do you store your guitar in that Hummer or did you put it in there so that you could play it?"

"You're not going to answer that, are you?" At the negative shake of her head he said, "I thought I might play it."

"Why don't you then? Take your mind off your troubles."

Jason gave a small nod. Lainey watched him walk back to the truck, admiring his fine ass as he did so.

Chapter Seven

Jason didn't even know if he could play. His cock was in charge of things at the moment. He wanted to fuck Lainey so bad, he hurt. He'd have been better off hiking. At least then all that he'd have had to remember would've been one foot in front of the other.

Back on the blanket he crossed his legs, and took the guitar out of the case. Propping it in his lap, he then set his fingers on the neck. He hesitated, his other hand poised over the strings. "I haven't played in, like, six years. It's probably gonna be pretty bad."

Lainey smiled. "I bet it's like riding a bike. Play for me."

Jason strummed a few chords. "Is there a pick in there?" he asked, craning to look into the case.

She picked one out and handed it to him.

"My fingers used to be so callused. Sometimes I didn't even use one. My fingers used to bleed on stage and I didn't even care."

Her encouraging smile slipped a little.

Jason decided to play one of his songs for her. It took him a few seconds to remember it all. It *had* been a long time. He was a little rusty. His fingers moved faster than his brain—like muscle memory, they knew what to do before his mind could catch up. He didn't sing, just played her the melody. He got so wound up in it that he didn't even see her reaction. Until he'd finished.

When Jase finally opened his eyes, Lainey sat there staring at him as if she'd never seen him before, tears streaming down her face. "You have such a gift. With that voice and the way that you put your heart into the music how could you just stop? Did it not break your heart to give up something that you so obviously love?"

"Don't cry," he said, reaching out to wipe a tear from her cheek.

Facing him, she moved closer. "Then you don't cry," she said, swiping a tear from his own cheek.

Mopping at his cheek, Jase was astounded—he hadn't realized that he'd even become emotional. He never cried. Playing the music used to be such a part of him. They'd done the same material night after night so that it had taken all the pleasure right out of it. He'd forgotten how much he loved it.

"It must have been some epiphany for you to have given this up." She searched his face.

"I didn't like all the stuff that came with it. It wasn't really a difficult choice at the time. I guess subconsciously I must have made the decision long before the rest of me caught up to it. Maybe not the teaching part, but quitting. I'd been thinking about it," he said, placing his hand back to her cheek. Leisurely he stroked his thumb back and forth along her skin.

Her gaze searched his.

"I mean don't get me wrong, I was grateful—am grateful for all the things that it provided me. But I didn't like me. But evidently," he huffed, "I miss the music."

"Why did you feel that you had to give one up for the other? The music for the teaching?"

"I guess I didn't really do it consciously. I was just so busy going to school and—" He had been about to say outrunning the press. "Looking long term that I just forgot how much I love it."

"So why didn't you combine the two and become a music teacher?"

"Huh, I never thought of that one."

"Why history?"

"I've just always been fascinated by it. And you know that saying 'doomed to repeat itself'. But I guess because

I'm a storyteller. I write my heart in song."

"You write your own songs too?"

"That was mine."

"Ohhh. Play something else."

"But you don't even know my stuff."

"That's okay. I'll get to know it."

"Well, how 'bout we find something that you know?"

"I'm kind of a country girl," she said, giving a little shrug of her bare shoulder.

"Mmm, okay, how about..." He started playing *Sweet Home Alabama* and when he got to the chorus he started to sing.

The pleasure on her face made him also remember what an audience had made him feel. To have a hundred and eighty thousand fans singing his own words back to him was an indescribable feeling. There was nothing like it. A high all of its own.

"Join in. Sing with me."

She shook her head.

He stopped playing. "Come on."

"No, I can't sing."

"I heard you this morning. You can so."

"That was with a bunch of other people and the organ blaring. I can't sing in front of someone that sings like you."

"Why not? I heard you. I think we'd sound good together."

She shook her head again.

"I won't play unless you sing with me. Okay, how about this one? He played the first few chords before beginning to sing Kid Rock and Sheryl Crow's *Picture*—a duet of sorts and about as country as Jason could get. It wasn't really his genre. "You know it?" he asked, while continuing to play.

She nodded.

When it was Sheryl's part, Lainey took his cue, timidly at first, but as he started to smile it must have encouraged her and her voice grew stronger.

They got to the duet part and they sounded great together, just as he'd known they would. He hit the last note, and

Lainey's cheeks reddened.

An abrupt spontaneous burst of applause caught them both off guard. Jason had thought they were in a secluded little patch where they wouldn't be disturbed or bother anyone else. He hadn't thought Lainey's face could get any redder than it already was. He was wrong.

"Thank you, thank you very much," he called with a little Elvis-style lip curl, waving to the small crowd of onlookers. "We'll be here all week," he joked.

"That was awesome, Lainey," he said, laying the guitar on the blanket. He wrapped his arms around her. "We sounded great."

"You sound great."

"No, we did." She had a natural voice, kind of an alto with a little rasp to it. If she practiced or took lessons she'd be awesome.

Lainey pulled from his embrace as the little crowd moved on. She picked up a sandwich and plunked it in his lap. After opening the grapes, she popped one into her mouth.

"So your parents live nearby then?"

He looked at her as she changed the subject again. "Yeah, they live in Jacksonville."

"And you go there for Sunday supper?"

"Yeah, my mom said that's what she missed most about me being on the road. She missed feeding me and knowing that I was eating well. When does a parent finally quit worrying or taking care of their kid?" He took a bite of the ham sandwich with lettuce and cheese.

"I don't think I'll ever quit worrying about Jilly. And I'm afraid the time is coming when she's not going to need me to take care of her. I sort of dread the day she goes off to college. We kinda grew up together. I mean, I want her to go and do everything she wants to, but I'm afraid for her too. I will always want to protect her from, well, everything I guess."

"She's a great kid, Lainey. She's going to be just fine."

Flipping onto her stomach, Lainey then rested on her

elbows with her legs bent and her bare feet in the air.

Jason followed the line of her leg until it disappeared into her shorts. Just the barest tease of the roundness of her shapely butt peeked where her shorts ended.

He grabbed her ankle. "Ah-ha, I did see a tattoo." He held her foot so that he could look at it. "The number twenty-two. You don't strike me as a tattoo kinda girl, Lainey. Did you get this while you were drunk? And what does it mean?"

"I wasn't drunk." She looked away, laying her head down on her arms. "It was Thad's number back in high school."

"Oh," he said, wishing that he hadn't asked. Thad and Lainey hadn't just been married, they'd been together all the way back in high school — the classic high school sweethearts. That was a lot of history.

"I thought about having it removed but" — she shrugged — "it makes me remember him the way he was and not the way that he ended up. I hate the Thad that shows up every once in a while to bring his daughter home or to serve me with more papers."

"But you were in love with the kid that wore jersey twenty-two."

Disregarding the statement, she shrugged again. "Besides, Jilly was born on the twenty-second, so I just left it. Don't tell me you don't have any tattoos. There's no way that you were in a band without them."

"That's just a cliché, a stereotype."

She sat up and slid a finger up his T-shirt sleeve and she grinned as she revealed at least one. "And you have the stereotypical tribal arm band that every guy of a certain age group has." She pushed his sleeve higher, while tugging at the other. "What else ya got?" She pulled at the bottom of his tee releasing it from his shorts. "Let me see."

He stopped her. "I'll take off my shirt if you take off yours." He grinned.

"What, ya got a girl's name on you that you don't want me to see? Maybe some naked woman?"

"No. But tit for tat, baby, you show me yours." He grinned evilly while pulling lightly on the elastic holding her peasant blouse off her shoulders. "And I'll show you mine.

"I already showed you mine," she said unable to keep a straight face.

"Nah-uh. You know exactly what I mean. You show me your tits and I'll show you my tats."

"Why, Mr Westlake, I cannot believe that you would use that kind of language. Do you use that mouth when you teach your students?"

He lowered himself until his face was just a whisper from hers. "I'm not Mr Westlake here, I'm just Jase and you're just Lainey and do you really wish for me to tell you what this mouth can do? Or better yet I'll show you."

Still sticking to his bargain, he didn't kiss her mouth. But he'd never said that he wouldn't kiss her elsewhere. He kissed his way over her jaw, brushing his lips softly across her ear.

"Ahh, Lainey," he whispered. "I wanna taste you." His words and his warm breath teased her skin, sending goose bumps skittering down her arms. With his tongue he traced around the outside curve of her ear right down to her lobe where he tucked his tongue between it and her neck. He flicked it softly yet quickly in the little nook, inciting shock waves of desire right between her legs. She wanted to feel his tongue there, flicking her clit.

Scoring her jaw with his teeth, he then gently eased her head back, exposing her throat. He kissed his way down, nipping at her collarbone before softly sucking the swell of her breast bared by her blouse. Lainey pulled the elastic of her shirt lower, encouraging him to continue. She'd never been one to verbalize what she wanted but she could certainly guide him. She thought she would scream if she didn't soon feel his lips close around her nipple. It tingled and hardened.

Jase followed the line of the blouse with his tongue. She wound her hands into his hair holding him to her. He fitted his hands around her breasts, kneading them. She arched her back, pushing her tits more fully into his palms. They were a perfect fit. He circled his thumbs around the stiff buds. "I wanna touch you, Lainey. I wanna kiss you. But not out here in the open. Let's go home."

"Ohh," she whimpered shakily, clinging to him. He had her so wrapped up in a sensual haze that she didn't care if they were out in public. She wanted to feel his lips, his tongue. She needed him to come inside her and fuck her until she couldn't think. Clamping her legs together, she almost groaned at the delicious pleasure the action produced.

He stood and reached down to her.

"Hey, Dub, is that you?"

"Oh, fuck!" Jason said, turning his back on whoever had called to him.

Lainey also twisted, pulling her top up. The interruption curbed her arousal in a hurry, but not his. Lainey grinned as Jason shoved a hand into his pocket trying to conceal the massive hard-on he sported.

"I thought that was you. I told Boy-o that was your Hummer in the lot."

"Hey, boys, what's up?" Jason's voice sounded raspy but Lainey thought it was very sexy.

"Hope we didn't interrupt ya, Teach," Boyd said.

Henry pointed to the woman sitting with her back to them on the blanket and raised his eyebrows rapidly and mouthed, "*Is that her?*"

Both boys waited, wide-eyed.

Jason nodded, knowing he was only setting himself up for more ribbing. But what could he do?

The teens broke out in broad knowing smiles.

"Havin' a nice little picnic, are we?"

"Well, we just wanted to say hey," Henry said, taking his

cue to leave. "We'll let ya get back to whatever it was you were...doin'." Kids were too freakin' smart for their own good.

Boyd snorted. Henry elbowed him. "Yeah, we just wanted to say hello, maybe introduce ourselves to your date. She might like to meet some of your students, don't ya think, Teach?"

Well, there was no dignified way to get out of this. Lainey must have realized it too. She patted her hair and stood up, adjusting her top before turning. Cheeks blazing, she looked directly at the boy she knew. "Hey, Henry, nice to see you again."

Henry's mouth dropped open and his face then bloomed with color.

"Mrs Markham, uh, yeah, hey," he said, looking off over her shoulder, unable to meet her gaze.

Boyd's eyes narrowed, as he must have recognized the name. "Hey, yeah, you're Jill's mom. Boyd Tanner." The cocky kid stuck out his hand, introducing himself.

Lainey smiled tightly, and shook it.

"Well, we'll let ya get back to it," Boyd grinned at the other three uncomfortable people.

"See you tomorrow, fellas," Jason said, following them a short distance, as if making sure they were actually leaving.

Boyd pulled up short and said out of the corner of his mouth. "Ya could've at least sprung for a room, Dub."

"Boyd!" he warned.

The kid shrugged. "Just sayin', man, anybody could walk by and see—"

"Shut the fuck up, Boyd," Henry said, between his teeth as he dragged him away by the shirtsleeve.

Jason took his hand out of his pocket and ran both hands through his dark hair, then over his face, before looking back at Lainey. But when he did they both burst out in embarrassed laughter. Lainey wrapped her arms around his waist.

"This is going to be all over school by tomorrow," Lainey

moaned.

Jason pulled her head against his chest. "Don't kid yourself. Boyd's probably already posted it on the latest social media site and by now fifteen kids have 'liked' it."

"Well, just as long as I get to tell Jilly before she sees it or someone else tells her. I can just imagine what four letter words he used to describe what they just saw." She rolled her eyes.

"Like what? Lick? Kiss? Suck? 'Cause that's all they saw. Luckily I stopped you before they—"

"*You* stopped *me*, did you? Before they could see the impressive four letter word you were trying to conceal with your hand in your pocket?"

"Impressive?" He grinned.

"Well, it definitely feels impressive."

"Oh, baby, you just wait."

"Can we go home now?"

"You bet." He jumped and started throwing the leftover food into the cooler.

They practically ran back to the Hummer.

They drove toward town. "Your place or mine?" Jason asked.

"Yours."

He nodded as Lainey's cellphone started to ring.

Lainey dug in her purse for it. Placing it to her ear, she answered, "Hello?"

"Where are you? Your car is here and I was freaking out. I came in the house and you aren't anywhere to be found. I looked all over. I thought you…"

"Slow down, Jilly, I'm fine."

"Well, where are you? Your car is here."

"You're home?"

"Fuck!" Jason threw his head back against the headrest in disappointment.

"What was that?"

"Nothing. Did you just get home?"

"Yeah, where are you?"

"I'm with a friend. I'm on my way home, though. I'll be there in about ten minutes."

"Who are you with?"

"We'll talk when I get home. Love you." She ended the call before having to answer any more questions.

Jason looked sideways at her in the passenger seat. "I guess that means I'm dropping you off at home?"

"I'm sorry, Jason."

"Not half as sorry as I am."

Not long after, Jason pulled the H3 into Lainey's driveway. Jumping from the truck, he ran around to open her door and give her a hand down.

Lainey was still a little shaky. Jason felt her tremble when she took his hand to step down. He liked knowing that he had her as rattled as she had him. He opened the back, took the cooler out and set it outside the front door for her. He turned, taking a deep breath.

"I guess I'll go."

"Thank you for a great day," she said.

"You too."

He leaned down and kissed her cheek, but this time she turned to him at the last minute. He stilled as she kissed his lips then pulled away, only to return for another and another before sinking into a real deep kiss. Sighing, he savored the taste of their first real kiss. Lainey curled her arms around the back of his neck as she stretched, flattening her breasts out against his chest. God, she felt incredible. He cupped his hands around her sweet little ass and pulled her against his eternal hard-on. She gasped. He seized the opportunity to tease her lower lip with his tongue, sweeping it deeply into her mouth. She met him, thrusting and sliding sensually.

Groaning, he pulled free. "God, Lainey, stop, you're gonna drive me crazy. I can't take it. I feel like I've had a hard-on for days."

Dazedly, she looked up at him. "Wow!" She breathed

heavily.

"Yeah. Wow! Kiss me like that again and—"

He didn't get to finish before she attacked his lips again, giving him the most raw hungry kiss he'd ever been lucky enough to receive. It was all open-mouthed teasing.

She whimpered and tilted her hips forward like she needed to feel his hardness pressing more firmly against her. It only accomplished driving him even closer to doin' her right here and now. There would be no sweet seduction. Just fuck, come, sleep, do it again. Her hips were driving him insane. He realized he was rocking and she was meeting him thrust for thrust. They were like two horned up teenagers saying goodnight on her mother's porch.

Abruptly, she looped her foot around the back of his leg. She shifted, leaning slightly backward, bringing her heat in contact with his straining shaft. He could feel the sweet warmth and imagined how slick and ready she must be. As soon as he backed her against the door frame he pulled her ass more firmly into his hands, then coaxed her other leg around his hip.

"Ahhh," he tore his lips from hers. "Let me in."

She didn't know if he meant inside her or the house. Either way, she wanted him there too. She was so hot and wet. But there was something that she was supposed to be remembering.

Just then the door opened.

Jason dropped her guiltily and turned away.

Lainey tried to make her legs work and hold her own weight. She looked at her daughter who stood with her mouth hanging open. Then her eyes snapped with anger, then hurt. "Well, isn't this interesting. Both my parents are sluts."

She slammed the door. Lainey jumped at the suddenness of the noise. But then anger kicked in. Slut! She thought not. She'd been with one man her entire life. Being with someone else was all very new to her. And she didn't need her daughter to accuse her of being loose just because she was going on with her life when Thad was the one that had screwed things up.

Lainey put her hand on the doorknob, determined to give her daughter a good talking to when Jason took her elbow.

"Don't go off on her."

"Why the hell not? I have never given anyone reason to call me such a thing, especially my own daughter."

"She's hurt, Lainey. She's obviously never seen her mother with anyone but her father. And I'm her freakin' teacher, for Christ's sake. That's gotta be weird. We said it ourselves. Granted it might have been better if you'd had a chance to tell her before she saw us together, but at least now she knows. Do you want me to come in with you and we'll talk to her together?"

"No, I don't think that would be a good idea right now."

Running his hand over his mouth, he then nodded. "I guess I should go. Can I call you later?"

At her nod, he gave her a quick kiss on the cheek.

She watched him climb into the Hummer and drive away before she went inside.

"What the hell are you doing?" Jill shrieked as soon as she opened the door.

"I was going to talk to you—"

"He's my freakin' teacher."

"You told me to ask him out."

"But I never thought you would."

"No, you thought I'd never be with anybody again."

"Neither did you, Mom, face it."

"Things have changed."

"Yeah, I can see that. The whole fuckin' neighborhood saw that things have changed. It's not bad enough they used to see all the whores Dad traipsed in and out of here, they have to watch PDAs from you and my fuckin' history teacher?"

"Watch your mouth. And he's just one man. There will not be a parade like there was with your father."

"How the hell am I supposed to face him tomorrow morning?"

"The same way you always have. This is not about you, Jill. He's not going to treat you any differently. So neither should you. Yeah, it might be a little weird and awkward for a while but soon he won't be your teacher—"

"Yeah, and then I'll be running into him in the kitchen in his boxers!" She flounced out of the room dramatically.

Lainey pictured that very thing. Jason in boxers... And that's as far as she got.

* * * *

Lainey sat at the kitchen counter reading the paper when Jill stormed back in with her laptop.

"As if you didn't make things awkward enough, look what Boyd Tanner tweeted for the whole wide world to see."

Just saw Westlake and his breast girl, er, I mean best, parkin' at the park. JW is alive and well and still has the moves! Rock on, Teach!

"Breast girl? I don't understand."

"Yeah, you wouldn't! How could you do this? As if we weren't dragged through the press backwards before, you have to go making out all over town with my fuckin' teacher? What's wrong with you? I expect that shit from Daddy but not you."

"It was an accident being seen at the park. And it's not the press that's spreading the gossip."

"No, worse, my classmates knew all about your business before I did. As if Lisa and Tammy didn't give it to me plenty the other day when they saw you 'having coffee', now the whole school is gonna get in on it. How long has this been going on?"

"Well, seriously only a couple of days."

"So since you went for my interview?"

"Well, no, not even then. At least not for me."

"So he's been into you since then? Is that what you're saying?"

Lainey shrugged. He'd definitely been the aggressor.

"So, you've known him, say, what, five days and you two are practically humping on the front porch for all to see?"

"Jill..." Lainey warned.

"So, I'm supposed to take it slow with boys but you can climb into anyone's bed—"

"Stop it right there. I am not going to discuss this with you. I am an adult, Jill, and I do not have to answer to anyone."

"Just like Dad. You two can do whatever you want, but you expect me to be a good girl. Great role models I have."

"Face it, you are a good girl. It's not just me that keeps you on the straight and narrow, Jill. You know how to handle yourself. You are your own best conscience. I'm proud of the girl you are."

"I wish I could say the same."

"Did you expect me to live the rest of my life alone?"

Jill laughed but it wasn't a humorous sound. "Don't pin the rest of your life on Jason Westlake. He's not the settle down, white picket fence type. He'll eat you up and spit you out and leave you in a pathetic heap just like Dad did. You have no idea who he is or what you're getting into."

"What does that mean? And what happened to *Mr Westlake's not like Dad. He's a nice guy?*"

"You'll figure it out. And it won't take twenty years this time." Jill turned on her heel, taking her laptop and leaving Lainey staring after her. *What did she mean?* Lainey really didn't know anything about Jason. Maybe she was jumping into this too fast. She wasn't thinking with her brain—her body had taken over and it was leading the charge. But for once she didn't want to lead with her brain. She wanted Jason Westlake. And maybe for once she'd worry about the consequences later.

* * * *

Jason turned over and punched his pillow. He couldn't sleep and it wasn't just the raging desire that pumped through his veins that kept him from resting. Lainey hadn't called. Why hadn't she? Jill had told her. That's what had happened. Jill had told her who he was and now she never wanted to see him again. She figured he was no better than her lousy ex.

Jason got up, showered and dressed for the day. It was casual Monday whether they liked it or not. It didn't feel like a three-piece suit kind of day. He dressed in his favorite worn jeans and a school T-shirt. He gathered up all the papers he'd neglected over the weekend and headed out of the door.

He stopped for coffee but Lainey didn't. Exiting the shop, he looked across the road but the store was in darkness. Neither was her car parked down the street. He went to school and faced the much dreaded razing from the pubescent throngs.

Chapter Eight

Jason walked into his classroom. Jill wasn't seated at her desk. That was different. She was always in class. Always there before he was. He tossed his briefcase on his bureau and put the coffee he didn't even want off to the side.

"Hey, Dub, how was your weekend?" Boyd called from the back of the room.

"I believe you already know how my weekend went, Mr Tanner, and then with all the class that you possess you tweeted all about it."

"Yeah, buddy! Saw your weekend with my own eyes. How'd it go after we left?"

"None of your business. My life outside of this school is off limits."

"Struck out, huh?"

Jason threw himself into the chair behind the desk and waited for the bell to ring — tuning out the giggling and the jokes they were making at his expense.

Henry strode into class, past the desk and started down the aisle to his seat. "Good morning, Henry," Jason said.

Henry turned, gave him a cool once-over. "Hey," he replied. He sat down in his seat in a defiant slump. This day just kept getting better and better.

The bell rang. "Books. Open," Jason barked. "Two-oh-three."

If the stories buzzing around the classroom were only true, he'd made out a whole lot better over the weekend than he really had. The conversation died down, but when he looked up all the shining little faces smirked at him just waiting for the next off word so that they could nail him again.

"This is a different chapter. No more breasts, Mr Westlake?" Boyd snorted.

"Fuck off, Boyd," Henry lashed out. "Grow the fuck up."

"Guess who else didn't get any this weekend?" Boyd retorted.

"Watch your mouth in my classroom and let's get to work," Jason roared.

All quieted.

Just then there was a small tap on the closed door and Jill let herself in. She had a pink late slip in her hand and her cheeks were just as colorful as the piece of paper.

After gliding over to Jason's desk, she then tossed the piece of paper on it.

"Thank you, Miss Markham."

She didn't even look at him, turning to make her way to her own desk. But it didn't stop the snickering and lewd remarks.

"She can get away with anything now that her mother's banging the teacher."

"Told ya they were bumpin' uglies, Jill," Lisa said.

"There's no way his is ugly!" Tammy sighed.

"Okay, people, let's quit acting like a room full of teenagers and let's get to work."

"We *are* a room full of teenagers. What'd ya expect?"

"Yeah, and I'd appreciate it if for once you'd act like the young adults that you pretend to be. Page two-oh-three. *Now*. Mr Tanner you have lots to say today. Start reading."

"Jesus, Jill, tell your mom to give it up already before J-Dub goes completely mental."

Jason slammed his textbook down on his desk. Henry, who evidently had also had about all he could take, pushed Boyd right out of his chair and onto the floor. And Jill, who was plainly mortified, fled the room.

Jason was torn — he didn't know whether to go after Jill or stay and keep hold of his classroom. Boyd stood and made the decision for him.

"What the fuck's the matter with you, Henry? You've gone and lost your fuckin' mind too!" As he got up, Boyd gave Henry's shoulder a push in retaliation.

Jason strode down the aisle toward the combatants.

"Henry, take a walk. Take your books. Take Jill's stuff too." He hoped the kid would take the hint and go find and talk to Jill.

"You!" Jason pointed to Boyd as Henry stalked from the room. "Sit your ass down and keep your mouth shut until the end of class. Can you do that?"

"Yeah but—"

"Zip it!"

Jason walked to the front of the class and looked around the room, making eye contact with several of the students. "Page two-oh-three," he snarled. "Start there and read. *Silently.*"

* * * *

Henry found Jill sitting by her locker, her knees drawn up and her face buried in her hands.

"Hey."

She raised her head. "Hey." He was glad to see she was dry-eyed.

"Westlake wanted me to bring you your stuff." He dropped her bag next to her and slid down the lockers to sit on the floor beside her.

"Thanks. You'd better get back to class."

"He told me to take a walk."

"Then take a walk."

"Why are you being like this? I didn't do anything to you, Jill. I thought we had something going then all of sudden you've turned into a sulky little, well, I don't even know."

"I just don't need what you're trying to offer right now. I've got my own stuff to deal with."

"What is it you think I'm trying to offer you?"

"Oh, come on. You just want to get in my pants, just like every other boy, just like every other man," she sneered.

"Yeah, because before when we were hanging out, I was forever putting the moves on you. I was perpetually pressuring you. Forcing you to do things you didn't wanna do. Forcing myself on you. Right? I'm such a dog."

She glanced down the hall.

"And we've known each other for, what, three or four years now and you've seen me go through how many girlfriends? And I've hurt every single one of them," he continued sarcastically. "Treated them all like shit. Got every single one of them knocked up and left them high and dry. I'm such a fucker."

"You done?" she asked.

"No, I'm not fuckin' done! I'm pissed. What the hell's wrong with you? Is it 'cause I made the team? Is that it?"

She didn't answer. She wouldn't even look his way.

He stood up. "Forget it. I don't need what you're offering either." He started to walk down the hall.

"Henry?" Jill called. He just kept walking. "Henry!" she called louder and the sound of her voice made him stop and turn around. This time she was crying. His chest hurt to see her tears.

She walked toward him. He picked up his pace, and when she got to him she threw herself against his chest. "Oh, Henry, everything just sucks!"

He put his arms around her and held her. When she calmed he said, "It's going to get better, Jill. I promise. When my folks got divorced, it took a while, but honestly things are so much better now for everybody. I think my parents actually get along better now than they ever did when they were together."

Henry coaxed her back to the lockers, and they sat down.

"That's never going to happen with my parents. My mother hates my father for what he did. And so do I. But he's still my father and I just keep remembering what it was like before and I just can't understand why he would throw her away like that." Pausing, she tucked her hair behind her ear.

"My mom is the greatest. And now this thing with Westlake. I just don't want her to get hurt like that again. She'd come out even more bitter than she already is. How do I know he's not going to do the same thing to her? We all know what he was like when he was Jase West." Jill tossed her hands up in the air. "My mom doesn't even know about his past. And I know that I should tell her the truth but I don't want to tell her. I want her to be happy, but I don't know if she can be with him. What if I don't tell her what I know about him and then when she does find out, she's going to blame me for keeping it from her? And then I'll be just as bad as my dad, lying and hiding things from her. And what if I tell her and she doesn't even give this a chance and then maybe I screwed her out of having something really great with him? Gawd!" She elbowed the locker. "And they were making out on my front porch. I mean seriously going at it." She shuddered.

"Yeah, they were pretty, uh, uh, close when Boyd and I saw them in the park too."

"You were with him?"

"Yeah, I kept him from tweeting right away, but I knew as soon as he was out of my sight that he was going to post something. I'm sorry. I wanted to warn you too, but, well, we haven't been that close lately and I was afraid you might think I was just calling you up out of the blue to stir up shit."

"Not your fault. They were the ones carrying on in public for everyone to see. I feel like maybe it's my fault that she's even seeing him. I suggested she ask him out. But now that it really looks like it's happening, I wish I hadn't. What do you think of him? Westlake. Do you think he's changed?"

Henry shrugged. He'd suggested the same thing to Westlake. Before he answered that question he needed to talk to him. "I don't know. But I think you have to let your mom make her own mistakes. Just like parents have to do with us. You can't protect her from everything. And soon you'll be going off to school somewhere."

"I know."

The bell rang and other kids started to file out of the classrooms spilling into the hall.

"You goin' to second class?" Henry asked Jill.

"I should. But I don't want to hear what everyone has to say about my mom and Westlake."

"Well, maybe some other scandal will break out and they'll forget all about them. I guess I'll see you later," Henry said giving her a nod.

"Henry?" she called to him. "Thanks."

"Anytime."

He got about halfway down the hall when she yelled his name again. Pausing he waited for her to catch up. She looked up at him, then away. She swallowed. "You have my father's number."

"What?"

"The jersey they gave you, it was my father's number. When he was in high school. When he and my mom met."

"That's why you stopped wanting to be around me?"

"Yeah, I know it sounds stupid and crazy. But, I just..." She shrugged. "I know in my head that it doesn't even make any sense. But I can't help what I feel, Henry."

Westlake was right.

"So where does that leave us now, Jill? Do you want me to quit?"

"You'd do that? For me?"

"Yeah, I would. But even if I did and you still think that I could hurt you that way, things still aren't going to work out. Because you're never going to trust me regardless of whether I'm on the football team or not. It has nothing to do with the team or the number. It has to do with what you think of me. And it can't be too highly if that's what you think. And I can't figure out why, because I have done nothing to you that would ever lead you to believe that I'm like that. Like your dad. Or Westlake?"

Jill looked away again. Henry sighed and shook his head. He thought they'd had a breakthrough. She'd opened up in a big way.

She grabbed onto his arm. "Let's get out of here."

"What?"

"I don't want to be here. Can we just go somewhere?" In that moment, he would've done anything for her.

He scrounged around in his pocket. "Here. Take my truck keys. I've got something I gotta see to. And I'll meet you out there."

He ran down the hall, dodging and jumping around other students.

"Slow down, Henry!" Coach Anderson yelled. "Why can't you dangle like that out on the field?"

Henry ignored him and kept on going.

By the time he got to Westlake's classroom he was out of breath. Luckily, none of the second class students had filed in yet. He stepped in and closed the door.

Westlake looked up. "Henry. Did you find Jill?"

"Yeah. She's fine. I need to know if you're still going after this other woman. The one here at school? As well as seeing Mrs Markham, er, Clarkson."

"I'm not."

"Because I didn't mean to put that thought in your head by telling you to keep her in mind and that she was hot and all that. Jill's mom doesn't need to be jerked around again. If you're just playing with her while you're wheeling some other babe—"

"I'm not, Henry."

"Because I'll go over there and tell her myself exactly who you are and—"

"Henry! There is no one else."

"What?"

"It was always her. When I told the class that it was someone here at school, it was Lainey—Mrs Markham. I just wanted to throw everyone off because I knew that Jill was already taking some flak because someone saw us together at the coffee shop. But I met Lainey during Jill's interview. And I've been tied up in knots ever since. I didn't mean to upset Jill or have the whole school talking about us. I know that's not what either of them need right now. But I have no intention of hurting her."

"Yeah, must be a family trait. Jill's got me all tied up in knots too."

"You two talked?"

"Yeah, but we still need to do some more. But she told me what's eating at her."

"That's good, Henry. I'm glad to hear it."

"You're not going to ask me what she said?"

"No, that's between you and her."

He nodded. "I gotta go."

"Thanks for going after Jill."

"No problem. Thanks for letting me." He walked toward the door then turned back around. "She's not too sure about you, Teach."

"I know. She has her reasons. I get that. And she loves her mother and doesn't want her to get hurt. But we all have that in common. I don't want that either."

"Boy, can we pick 'em, eh, Dub? Couldn't pick simple women. No. Gotta go for the complex ones."

"I've come to the realization that the complex ones are the only ones that are worth it."

"Yeah, and you've tried them all out, one at a time, to come to that realization. And when Mrs Markham finds that out, well, let's just say I wouldn't want to be in your shoes."

"Well, hopefully by the time she finds out, she'll be too into me to just turn her back on me. I'm not Jase West anymore."

"Don't you think it'd be better just to come clean with her upfront? Just be honest? She needs honesty now after all Markham put her through. Not to mention, you're putting Jill in a helluva bad spot here, J-Dub. She knows who you are too and she doesn't know what to do. Should she tell her mom and ruin what might be a good thing between you two or just wait and let it ride and hope she's okay with it when she does find out?"

"She didn't tell Lainey last night?"

Henry shook his head.

Jason let that sink in. "Yeah, I know you're right. I guess that would be the right thing to do."

"It would also show that you're not Jase West anymore, that you have evolved."

"You're pretty smart, kid."

Henry grinned, for the first time since he'd walked in. "Yeah, the ladies love an intelligent guy."

The kids for second class started filing in. "Get outta here, I've got a class to teach."

"Later, Teach." Henry ran back down the hall and right out of the doors sprinting toward the parking lot.

Chapter Nine

Jason checked in at the office for any messages. It was three thirty and still not a word from Lainey. So if Jill hadn't ratted him out why hadn't she called? Had she changed her mind? She'd cooled off and realized she wasn't ready?

Jason slammed the file cabinet on his way past, causing the ladies in the office to jump. "Sorry, ladies."

Lainey was ready—more than ready. She was practically jumping him on the porch last night. So what the fuck had changed? Why hadn't she called?

"Hey, ladies, got a phone book?"

They rushed to find it for him, bumping into one another in their haste.

Jase gave them a smile. "Thank you."

Back in his classroom he threw it on his desk. He flipped through it. "Markham, Markham."

"Nothing. Probably unlisted. What about Clarkson?"

"Nope. I'll try the store."

"H, I, J." Jason ran his finger down the page. "There we go, Jillian's Boutique.

Jason pulled out his cell and dialed.

"Jillian's." When Lainey answered he closed his eyes at the sound of her cheery voice. "Lainey speaking. How may I help you?"

"You could tell me why you didn't call?"

"I was thinking the same thing about you. You said you would call me."

"No, you were supposed to call me."

"No, you said *can I call you later*? And I said yes."

"I did? No, I couldn't have, I don't have your numbers."

"I don't have yours either."

"You could have called the school."

"I wouldn't bother you at work, Mr Westlake. And you have access to Jill's file if you needed contact numbers."

"I cannot go into a student's file for personal reasons." He rolled his eyes heavenward. As if he hadn't gone into her file once before. As if he hadn't thought of looking in her file, *again*.

"Oh, then this is a personal call?"

"Lady, you are driving me insane. I've been going nuts all night long and all day wondering why you didn't call."

Lainey smiled. It was unbelievable how crazed he sounded. "You were supposed to call me."

"Well, I probably did say it, but my mind was elsewhere. I apologize."

"No need. I believe my mind was the same place as yours."

"Do you have to rush home tonight for Jill?"

"Actually I just got a text from her about half an hour ago. She said she's with Henry at his house and not to worry about her."

"Then can I interest you in joining me for supper this evening?"

"What did you have in mind?"

"I'll meet you at five."

"All right."

"Great."

"See you then."

She was about to hang up when his deep rasping voice intoned, "Lainey... I can't wait."

As she hung up she couldn't help but grin like an idiot. Every time she thought of him, she felt warm and tingly all over. She had a permanent heaviness between her legs just in waiting anticipation of what could happen between them. She'd never experienced this kind of wild lust. Even when she and Thad had been teenagers she'd never experienced this incredible sexual need. When they'd first started having sex, she'd done it to please Thad and out of her own curiosity, of course. But it had hurt, and she hadn't got anywhere near the same amount of pleasure out of it that he had seemed to. But it had got better as they'd got used to each other and older. Lainey finally realized that she could seek out some pleasure in the act too.

The phone rang again, pulling her from her reverie.

"Jillian's. Lainey speaking. How may I help you?"

"Give me your cell number."

"Don't you ever say *hello*?" she laughed, and rhymed off her cell number for Jason, then asked for his. She programmed it into her phone under Jase. That's how he introduced himself to other people. But he hadn't with her. She wondered why.

Jason couldn't wait to get out of the school. In a much lighter mood, he returned the phone book. He headed straight to the grocery store. Lainey liked Italian and he knew how to make a mean spaghetti sauce.

Once home, he set the sauce to simmering then went for a shower.

At about four forty-five his cellphone chimed.

Running a little late. Sorry.

No problem, he texted back. *Meet me at my place when you're ready?*

K. Need your address, she responded.

He texted it to her.

See you soon.

About a minute later she sent, *I can't wait either.*

Jason smiled. He couldn't remember ever being this excited about seeing a woman. He'd never even cooked for one before.

While he waited impatiently, he chilled some wine and set the table.

Half an hour later when he saw Lainey pull into his drive, his stomach leaped and so did other things. Dropping the pasta into the boiling pot, he then set the timer for nine minutes, and rushed to the door.

After she knocked he counted to ten so she wouldn't know he was practically waiting at the door.

When he opened it and saw her standing there his heart pounded.

She smiled. "Hi."

He yanked her inside. "Hello." Then slid his hands into her hair and pulled her lips to his, while kicking the door shut. Half expecting timidity, to his delight she picked up just where she'd left off the day before — kissing him hungrily, raw and fierce. Straining to get closer she clutched at his hips.

Jason cupped her backside and drew her against him, lifting her off her feet. He dropped his hips and thrust upward giving her a sample of what he wanted to do to her. Backing her against the door, holding her, he coaxed her legs around his hips. Full skirt and all, she wrapped her legs around him, using her muscles to cinch him closer. It felt so good his hardness pressing into her softness. An animalistic sound rumbled from his chest, followed by a delightful moan from Lainey. In an attempt to breathe, he ripped his mouth from hers.

"Now," she cried. "Please, now!"

Jason stilled, his mind slow. She looked so fuckin' good, her eyes pained with desire and need. With Lainey still clinging to him, he staggered over to the couch and lowered her onto her back. Frantically she went straight to his waistband struggling with the snap and zipper of his jeans. When she'd managed to get them undone she pushed at the denim. He grabbed the hem of her skirt and bunched it up around her waist. He leaned back enough so that he could look down at her—little white bikini type panties greeted him. He palmed the triangle between her legs, his thumb abrading the furrow, sliding up to circle her clit through the cotton. Crying out again, she arched her back and undulated her hips.

Jason gripped her panties and dragged them down her legs then tossed them carelessly aside. He looked down at her again. Her beautiful hairless pussy beckoned him. "Ahhh, fuck, Lainey!" he exclaimed at the sweet surprise, his cock throbbing painfully. He wanted to bury his face between her thighs, slide his tongue into her sweet wetness. He cupped his hands under her ass, lifting her slightly, tipping her forward, having every intention of licking her.

"I don't need that. Please! I-need-to-feel-you-inside-me," Lainey all but moaned incoherently running the whole sentence into one big word.

He didn't need to be told again. But he didn't have a condom on him. *Fuck!*

"Just give me a sec. Don't move."

Helplessly, she whimpered.

Jason sprinted for the stairs, taking them two at a time, holding his jeans up so he wouldn't trip. He skidded into his bedroom and pulled a string of condoms out of the box in the drawer at his bedside. He pushed his boxers aside, before tearing one of the foil packets open with his teeth then rolling it on. As he would expect of one of his randy students he ran undignified, back down the stairs to the soft beautiful woman waiting for him.

With her skirt still rucked up around her waist, she opened her arms to him. Stepping out of his jeans and boxers he joined her on the sofa then kneed her legs open wider. He ran his fingers between her pussy lips and groaned at the wet warmth he felt there. She was so ready for him. She scooched down the couch, getting closer as he guided his heat-seeking cock into her.

Lainey was disappointed to see the condom. Of course, it

was the right thing. They barely knew each other and she knew absolutely nothing about his history. But she wanted to feel him. All of him. His skin in hers. The second he rubbed the throbbing tip of his cock through her slick cunt, she no longer cared. Pressure and deep penetration were all she craved. Her body was on fire.

Jason plunged forward burying himself to the hilt—at long last filling the bottomless fiery yearning he'd been stoking in her since they'd met. She opened her mouth on a silent moan of pleasure and relief.

As he looked down at her, he began to move. Lainey cupped each of his butt cheeks, encouraging his frantic pace. She splayed her legs wider giving him full access.

"Ahh, Lainey. God, you feel so good."

Lainey was shocked at how amazing it felt. Generally she wasn't able to come this way, needing clitoral stimulation to get there. But she was so close. His cock abraded just the right spot. Then sweet spasms began to build way deep down inside her. "Ohh, Jay-sonnnnn," she moaned as one delectable wave of pleasure after another crashed over her.

Her pussy contracted around the base of his shaft, tightening and squeezing him, pulling him deeper. Constant overlapping tremors made her inner walls ripple enticingly. She felt so fuckin' sweet. "Aww, Lainey, I'm comin' already," he confessed on a long quaking shudder. He ground into her until he felt himself losing substance.

Pulling out, he then eased down beside her. Her eyes were shining and bright. Something inside his chest squeezed at that look.

"Wow!" She smiled up at him lazily.

"Yeah. Wow! You little volcano!"

She giggled. Jason ran a hand over her hip, needing to touch her.

"Do I smell something burning?"

"Oh shit!" Jason jumped up and ran into the kitchen.

The room was full of smoke. The pasta had almost boiled dry. It was all stuck to the bottom of the pan. Taking it off the burner, he then set it in the sink, and flipped on the exhaust fan over the stove. He yanked the cord for the ceiling fan above the dining table.

Lainey entered the kitchen. "What happened?"

"I forgot that I put the pasta in as soon as I saw you drive in."

"Why didn't you set the timer?"

"I did. But I was slightly distracted. I didn't hear it."

"I didn't hear it either," she confessed. "Well, that's quite the look you got going on there." Her gaze traveled over him. He wore a worn T-shirt, a condom and a pair of socks. Yeah, he must've presented quite the picture. "Maybe you should put these back on before you burn something important?" she suggested, smiling, holding up his jeans with one finger through a belt loop.

Jason turned slightly and rolled the condom off then tossed it in the garbage under the sink. Accepting the jeans from her he then slid into them.

Lainey looked into the other bubbling pot on the stove. "What have we got here? This still smells good." She leaned over the low simmering tomato sauce and took a long sniff of the aroma. "Let's just cook some more pasta. I'll try to keep you from being distracted." She sidled up to him, standing close but not touching him. Then she kissed his chin.

Sliding an arm around her, he pulled her against him. "And how do you intend to do that? Just you being here has me distracted." He dropped a kiss on her nose.

"I could leave." Half-heartedly, she made an attempt to turn.

"No fuckin' way." He tightened his arms around her.

She wound hers around his neck. "Maybe if we watch the pot together, we'll keep each other on task."

"A watched pot never boils."

"Sure it does. Good thing you're not a science teacher."

"At the moment I'm thinking biology. Yours as it relates to mine."

"You are easily distracted, aren't you?"

"You are an incredibly distracting woman."

They were so close that when her stomach growled he felt it as if it were his own.

"I'm a hungry woman." She laughed softly, her breath brushing his chin.

Only intending to give her a quick peck, Jason leaned down and kissed her gently but the soft supple give of surrender under his mouth had him sipping from her sweet lips over and over until they were both breathless. A new torrent of pure lust pounded through him. But her stomach rumbled again. Reluctantly he dragged his lips from hers. "I guess I'd better feed you first."

Dazedly Lainey looked up at him.

Jason set her away from him and filled another pot with salty water. He placed it on a burner to boil. "What's with the raucous little lion in there?" Delicately he tweaked her tummy.

"I didn't get away for lunch today."

"Oh, busy day?"

"No, unfortunately."

"No? So, why couldn't you run across the street and get some lunch?" he asked, stirring the sauce.

"I didn't want to leave the phone," she admitted looking down at the floor. He grinned slightly. "Just in case you called," she added quietly.

He liked knowing she was waiting by the phone for him to call.

After dropping the pasta into the pot, he hauled her back into his arms. "I fucked up. I'm sorry. And now you're starving and it's all my fault."

"That's okay, you're making up for it now." She lifted her lips for a kiss and he obliged.

"I'll make it up to you," he said, pulling her against his burgeoning erection.

Lainey ran her hand down the hardening length. "Mmm," he murmured appreciatively, pushing himself fully into her palm. "Keep that up and I'll boil dry another batch of pasta."

She removed her hand. "Oh, well, we wouldn't want that now, would we?"

Jason grabbed her wrist and flattened her palm, then wrapped her fingers around his stiff cock. She molded them around him and followed his shaft down, where she then cupped his balls firmly through worn denim. "Yeah, I wouldn't mind at all. Who needs pasta anyway?" He wound his hands into her hair and tugged her head back. Lowering his mouth he kissed her with all the crazed fierceness he was feeling. She made him wild. She was all he could think about. All he wanted to think about. She was his newest obsession. The sweet little tease of hurried lovemaking earlier was not nearly enough to assuage the boiling in his blood.

She met him, though, gave as good as she got while palming him until he could think of nothing more than sinking into her. She caressed him with her tongue in the same rhythm that her hand was playing his cock. Stroking him from the outside of his clothes wasn't enough. As if she read his mind, she thumbed his jeans open, undid the zipper and slid her warm hand down his straining rod. He was throbbing, pulsing, jerking. It wouldn't take much for him to come right in her hand.

Lainey ripped her mouth from his—her eyes were wild, her chest heaving. Easing the hot pot from the burner she then turned off both elements, to the pasta and the sauce.

"Who needs to eat?" she panted, moving back into his arms.

Yes! his mind screamed. Scooping her into his arms he then carried her up the stairs to his bedroom. She turned her head and kissed wherever she could reach him—his jaw, his chin, his chest. At his bedside, he set her on her feet, capturing her mouth again. She pushed his jeans off his hips. They fell down around his ankles. She snaked a hand back around his thickness and continued to manipulate his hot flesh, tugging and pumping his cock until he could barely stand it. Gathering great folds of fabric, he pulled her skirt up and skimmed his hands over her smooth hips. The realization that she'd decided not to put her panties back on made him moan. "God, you were like this the whole time we were in the kitchen?" he asked. The thought of only the skirt between them made his cock vibrate in her hand. "Ahhh, God, Lainey, I woulda put you right up on the counter," he breathed heavily.

"And what?" she whispered back into his mouth. "What would you have done to me?"

"Ohhh, God. I woulda knelt between your beautiful thighs." He moved his hand between her legs and moaned again when he felt how slick she was. "I would have slid my tongue right up inside you. Tasted you." Demonstrating, he worked his finger between the luscious folds. She bore down on his finger and sighed into his mouth. Going deep, he pushed his fist against her, wiggling the digit unmercifully. His anxious plundering seemed to work for her. She moaned with pleasure, which only drove him closer to culmination. Ultimately, he wanted to taste her, but he wouldn't survive it and selfish as he was he wanted to be buried in her, where his finger now tickled and teased her.

His own hot juices churned just under the surface of his skin as she continued to tug and stroke him expertly. "I wanna be in you."

"I want you there."

He shuddered, trying to control himself, then edged her toward the drawer. "Can we get rid of this?" she demanded of his shirt.

With that out of their way, her gaze skipped from one tattoo to another but he didn't care. Jason went after the buttons on her dress. But silently, she lifted her arms, and he dragged the dress over her head. Just her bra stood in his way. He fumbled with clumsy fingers. Taking pity on him she undid the hooks. He helped her slide it down her arms. And he'd been completely right about being obsessed with those lovely breasts. Flawless. He took each one in hand. Her lips parted at his touch.

"Ah, Lainey, you're perfect," he murmured as he lowered his head. He captured one sweet bud in his mouth softly rolling his tongue.

She made the raspiest little erotic sound. "We have lots of time for that. I need you now," she whispered catching his chin in her palms.

He leaned toward the drawer to grab a condom.

"Do you need it? I'm clean. I had all the tests you can possibly have after I found out about, well, you know." She seemed reluctant to mention her ex's name, which Jason appreciated. "I want to feel you with nothing between us."

Oh God! So did he. But he couldn't put her at risk. He hadn't been careful. "Are you on the pill?" he stalled for time.

Her face fell. "No," she said, disappointed. Reaching into the drawer, Lainey then ripped open the packet. She was about to roll it on, then leaned down and placed a sweet kiss on the tip. He almost leaped out of his own skin at the thought of her lips wrapping around him. Involuntarily his hips thrust forward as she rolled the condom on.

Smoothing his palm down her arm he then backed her to the bed. When her knees caved he lowered her and followed her down, he levered himself above her and she guided his swollen cock into her.

Almost immediately, he felt the rolling wave of sweet contractions deep inside her hot tight pussy.

Deep and slow, he thrust once, twice. But it wasn't the speed he wanted to go just now. As she'd said, they'd have time for everything else later. When they weren't so hot and horny for each other. Right now, they both needed intense and fast. He picked up the pace as his heart pounded out of his chest and his blood rushed. A fine sheen of sweat broke out over his body.

"Ohh, Jaassooonnnn!" She pulled her legs back and reached for him. Her nails scoring him, she grabbed his ass, and encouraged his frenzied thrusting. Another amazing wave of spasms overtook her insides, making her close in around him. "Oh God!" she cried.

Oh God was right. Rocking against her, he exploded and emptied into the rubber. He eased himself down beside her, trying to keep them connected but as he deflated, it made it more difficult. But he wanted to enjoy the delicious little aftershocks she kept having. He pulled her into his arms — her to his chest. Like a satisfied little cat she stretched, molding herself to him as she continued to rock her hips against him. She ran her hand over his stomach and chest, up over his arm and shoulder, then back again. He could feel himself relaxing, close to sleep.

He woke when she stiffened beside him. "What is it?" he asked sleepily.

"I think I just heard my cellphone."

They listened. Seconds later in the distance they heard the alarm signaling a text.

"It's Jill," Lainey said and started to get out of bed.

"I'll get it." He stayed her arm. It would be easier for him to just slide into some pants and run than her having her dress. He pulled on a pair of pajama pants. "Where is it?"

"In my bag, probably by the door where I dropped it." She bit her lip and he knew she was remembering how they'd attacked each other when she'd first walked in. Yeah, that was hot.

After retrieving her purse he ran then back up to his room to find her still lounging in his bed with the sheet pulled up. He'd half expected her to be dressed. Pausing at the door for a moment he simply watched her. He liked seeing her in his bed.

He handed her the purse. "Thanks." She leafed through the bag and came up with a cell. Reading the text, she pouted slightly.

"Everything okay?" Jason fell into bed beside her and dropped a kiss on her bare shoulder.

"Yeah, Henry just dropped Jill off at home and she's wondering where I am." Lainey turned her lovely green gaze his way. "What should I say?"

"Mmm, I'm thinking telling her you're in my bed is not the appropriate response?"

"No," she answered.

"Have you talked to Jill today? I mean other than the couple texts?"

"No. Why?"

"Uh, we had a rough day at school today," he confessed. He didn't know how she'd take this.

"What do you mean?"

"Uh, our friend Boyd did just as I predicted and outed us on Twitter. The class was pretty brutal. Jill ran out..."

"She did? Why didn't you tell me that on the phone? I should have..."

"I sent Henry after her. I needed to stay and keep a cap on the class or I would have gone after her myself. But then again, maybe I'm the last person she would want to talk to or confide in right now. Since I seem to be the source of her angst at the moment."

"*We* are the source of her angst for the moment." She tossed the sheet aside. "I need to go. Which door is the bathroom?" she asked, looking around the room.

Jason pointed it out. Sighing heavily, he then placed his hands behind his head. Had he fucked up again? He'd never been with a woman with a kid. Let alone a teenage kid — a teenage kid who was his student. They were a breed all their own, he was learning. And the difference between the boys and the girls was like a chasm. But thankfully, Jill wasn't as dramatic as some of the girls. He hadn't been thinking about Jill when he'd called Lainey earlier. He'd had one thing on his mind. Maybe now that he'd got it, he'd be less selfish, but he didn't hold out much hope for that. It was foreign to him to put someone else first. And he knew now that if he'd led off the conversation on the phone with Lainey earlier with *Jill ran out of class*, Lainey would not have just left his bed now. Her first priority was her daughter. Not him. That might take some getting used to.

Lainey strode out of the bathroom. All put back together. Just as neat as she'd been when she'd shown up at his door.

She stopped and looked at him. "Ohhh." She bit her lip. "I'm sorry." She sat on the edge of the bed. Bending over she kissed his chest, right beside the 'I heart Mom' tattoo. He resisted the urge to pull Lainey back into his bed.

"I need to go make sure she's okay."

He nodded. "I know. I'll walk you down."

Hand in hand they walked down the stairs. At the bottom she took a detour to the couch. With a wave of her panties, she then bunched them up and stuffed them into her oversized bag. She continued to surprise him. There was a little devil under that prim and proper mom act.

Jason rolled his eyes at the thought of her leaving here commando. "Ahh, Lainey," he breathed wrapping her back in his arms. "You can't tease a guy like that."

"Why not? You're not wearing anything more under there than I am." She scooted both hands down his pants then cupped his bare ass.

"But I'm not going outside. And you've got all those sweet little treasures hidden under that skirt." He lowered his head and took her lips, just as her phone went again.

She pulled it out and read. "She's hungry," Lainey said, indicating Jill's most recent text.

"It's too bad, I've got lots of food," he offered. "And I know you're hungry. What are you going to tell her, you know, about where you've been?"

"I haven't figured that out yet. I think I'll tell her I was with you. I just don't think I'll tell her that we were here."

Lainey looked up at him. "Will I see you tomorrow?" A worried gaze searched his. How could she even ask that? He didn't want her to leave right now. If he could wake up with her in his arms, that would be his idea of seeing her tomorrow. But he knew that this was her insecurity. That she wasn't sure of him yet. And it was to be expected after what she'd been through.

"Try to keep me away," he answered, kissing her again. When he let her go she maintained that dazed look. He knew that would fade with time, so he was going to savor it now while he had that effect on her.

She walked down the path, then turned and gave him a little wave.

He watched until she drove away, then closed the door. He went into the kitchen and drained the pasta. It was overcooked after sitting in the hot water for so long. So much for al dente. He tossed the pasta in with the sauce and stirred it all together. Then he stared at it. He hadn't intended to consume it alone.

Tossing a lid on it he then turned to put it into the fridge when he spied the takeout containers from Batallio's. Ever since the night that he'd been there with Lainey, he'd gone there for takeout. A perfectly devious plan took hold. Scooping out the cold food he then gave the containers a quick wash. He dumped his homemade spaghetti into the Styrofoam squares. He was taking his woman and her daughter some takeout.

Chapter Ten

Lainey walked in the door at home. It was quiet. "Hey, Jilly. I'm home."

"Hey, Mrs M."

Lainey jumped at the unexpected voice.

"Henry..." She turned to see the teenage boy who seemed entirely too grown up at the moment, walking out of the kitchen, looking way too comfortable doing so.

"Hey, sorry, didn't mean to scare you. Jill's just upstairs."

Lainey nodded, not quite knowing how she felt about Henry being alone with Jill. Her daughter had failed to mention that Henry was here with her. *Stop being a hypocrite*. She and Thad had been so much younger than Jill when they'd started having sex. And she didn't even know how close Jill and Henry were. Things had cooled off between them, but they seemed to be heating up again.

Lainey made her way up to her own room. She needed to make herself decent and change, at least put some underwear on. What had she been thinking? She was a mom for crying out loud. She pulled on a pair of shorts and a flowered tank top. Gathering up her hair, she gathered it into a sloppy bun. As she walked down the hall she met Jill on the stairs.

"Hey."

"Hey. You didn't tell me Henry was here."

"He hasn't been here the whole time. When you weren't here I texted him to come back." Jill continued down the stairs. "Where were you?" Then quieter she said, "As if I didn't know."

"Well, if you know then I don't need to tell you," Lainey

said, following her into the kitchen. She filled up the kettle and set it to boil.

"Didn't you bring anything to eat?" Jill complained.

"No. Last time I did you had supper made."

Jill slumped onto a stool. Henry sat down beside her. "We're starving," Jill continued.

Just as Lainey turned to give her a cool motherly stare, the doorbell rang. "You expecting someone else?" Lainey asked, looking between the two of them.

"No. But I sure hope it's spontaneous delivery," Jill grumbled.

Lainey padded to the door and opened it, gasping at the tall dark handsome teacher who'd just finished giving her two toe-curling orgasms. Her stomach leaped at the sight of him, as well as a sweet tingle down below.

"Hey," she said in surprise.

"Hey, thought I'd bring dinner, since we didn't get a chance to go out," he explained. Lainey stepped aside so that he could come in, glad that she hadn't gone into any details. Unexpectedly, he kissed her cheek with Jill and Henry looking on. It was a statement.

"Hey, Dub," Henry said. "Excellent timing. Jill's *starving*," he laughed teasing her. "Batallio's too. Isn't that your favorite?"

Jill shrugged.

Henry took the containers from Jason.

Lainey looked up at him. "What are you doing?" she rasped.

Taking her hands, he then pulled her close. "You look sexy as hell." He kissed the end of her nose. "I wasn't ready for our night to end. Besides you didn't get to eat and I invited you for dinner. And I believe I heard your daughter was also hungry. So, come on, while it's hot."

Jill watched them closely as, hand in hand, they approached the table.

"Hi, Jill."

"*Mister* Westlake. How did you know I was hungry?"

"Oh, excuse me, Miss Markham," Jason responded. "I didn't realize we were being so formal. Should I have dressed for dinner as well?"

"I don't remember you being invited for dinner, Mr Westlake," she answered frostily. "How did you know I was hungry?"

"Jill…" The steel in Lainey's rebuke brought about a stiff apology. "We were together when I got your text," Lainey justified, grudgingly.

"Oh. Have you been with him all this time? Since the shop closed?"

"Yes, when you messaged that you were at Henry's I figured I was on my own for supper, so we made plans."

"Plans?"

"Yes, dinner plans. As you can see."

Jill set out some plates, while Lainey provided some cutlery. "Coffee?" Lainey asked Jase.

"Whatever you're having. I'm easy," he grinned, holding her gaze.

She smiled then turned away, making them each an instant coffee.

"Want a soda, Henry?" Jill asked.

"Yeah, I'll get them," he said, helping himself.

Lainey opened one of the containers. Henry popped the other and they each served their partners.

"It smells weird," Jill complained. "Not like Batallio's at all."

"I think it smells fantastic," Lainey exclaimed, rolling the fork around the spaghetti. "I'm starving."

The phone rang.

Lainey got up to answer it. "Hello?"

"So," Henry sat back in his chair and examined Jason from across the table. Jase knew he was up to something. Henry put his arm around Jill's shoulders. "Jase. Is it Jason? Can I call ya Jason?" he asked, in a deep fatherly tone. "The little missus and I would like to know what your intentions are concerning our little Lainey there." The kid could barely keep a straight face.

"The little missus, Henry?" Jason watched the kid. "I wasn't aware that I needed to ask permission or make my intentions known. And Jason is fine."

Jill narrowed her eyes on him. "I'm perfectly aware of who you are. And that's exactly why I would like to know your intentions." Jill crossed her arms over her chest.

"Hey, Jill," Henry protested. "I was just foolin' around."

"Yeah, and so is he. My mother isn't the kind of person who fools around. If she's interested in you, then it's serious. It's not just sex to her, *Jase*."

"Hey, whoa, whoa, hey," Jason held up his hands. He'd never intended to get into this kind of conversation with them.

"My mother gave my father everything she had," Jill continued. "And he threw it all away. I never thought my mother would even look at another man, let alone what seems to be going on between the two of you. If you're just going to jerk her around, then walk away right now before you hurt her. It would be much easier for her to cope before things get much more hot and heavy. We know who you are and about your past and your reputation. You were no better than my father. She can't take it again. I won't let you hurt her."

"That's just it, Jill. I *wasn't* any better. But I'm not that guy anymore. I don't want to be that guy anymore. That's why I quit to become a teacher."

"Henry said he heard you singing yesterday. What if you go back to it? What if you can't stand to be the humdrum schoolteacher for long and you need to go back to the adoring crowds and the groupies. Then what?"

"Hey, Jill, ease up, they're just seeing each other," Henry attempted to reason with her. "We're not talking long term yet. What if your mom finds out he's the biggest jerk in the world? I mean she's pretty savvy. She might just have her fun with him then kick him to the curb. That's the way

I see this going. Jase West, puh-lease, not even in Lainey Clarkson's league."

Jill turned on him. "You think my mom's hot, don't you?"

"Well, you know what they say about apples and trees, right?" Henry grinned.

Jill frowned then she gave him a swat before turning back on Jase.

"He's probably right, you know," Jason said, trying to diffuse the snowballing situation. "She'll probably figure out that I'm the world's biggest jerk, but I'd sure appreciate the chance to prove you all wrong and maybe someday Jason Westlake will be worthy of being maybe not in the same league with Lainey Clarkson but maybe in the minors."

Jill opened her mouth to speak when Lainey hung up the phone and came back to the table.

"I hear you had a rough day at school today," Lainey said to Jill, as everyone dug into their meal.

"Where'd you hear that?" Jill asked.

"Jason said that you left class."

"Thanks," she said, giving him a derisive look.

"And," Lainey continued, "that was an automated message from the school. Apparently you did not attend school for the remainder of the day either. A student in your household..." she mimicked in a monotone.

Jill and Henry shared a look.

"And I take it by that little exchange, perhaps you were not alone."

"Henry and I cut. I was going to tell you. Preferably not in front of one of my teachers, but I was."

"I heard nothing," Jason said. "I left my credentials at home."

"Why did you leave school? There is nothing that people can say now that can hurt us. It's all been said, read about and played out for everyone to speculate. We've been gossiped about and judged before. Be thankful this is just frivolous school gossip, it's not plastered all over every tabloid rag or sensationalist 'entertainment' show. That's all over with. This is a breeze compared to before. This is all good stuff, Jilly. So what? I kissed your teacher. And I plan on kissing him again."

Jill's mouth dropped open and Henry grinned.

"So you and everyone else better get used to it. Some other scandal will come along and take over soon enough, and you can gossip along with the rest of them. The weekend is coming, someone will pull some bone-headed drunken stunt at a party and that will be all the buzz by Monday." She took a bite of her supper. "Mmm, this is really good." She looked around the table at the three people staring at her in various states of surprise. "What?"

Jill didn't answer, Henry grinned stupidly at her so she turned her attention to Jason.

"What are *you* grinning about?" she asked.

"I'm looking forward to you kissing the teacher again." Jason raised his eyebrows. "When might that be?"

"Ahhh, gross," Jill rolled her eyes.

"Well, not until you drop that cocky, shit eatin' grin, that's for sure," Lainey retorted.

Henry snorted and almost fell off his chair.

Lainey turned her attention to Henry. "So, Henry, what were you and my daughter up to all day?"

Instantly, he stopped laughing and nearly dropped a full fork. "We...we just talked...and stuff and drove around."

"And stuff?"

"No, I mean, we drove around and talked."

"And what did you do at your house?" Lainey asked, acting like it was just mild conversation, as she coiled spaghetti on her plate.

Henry gaped at Jill. But she kept her head down, not meeting anyone's gaze. She put a huge forkful of pasta into her mouth.

"Ahh, how the tables have turned, kid," Jason chuckled.

"We just played games and stuff, hung out."

"Was your mother at home?"

He made a choked sound. "No, she was at work."

"Mom, stop. Enough with the third degree. We just hung out. I was going to tell you."

Lainey gave them both the once-over.

"Now…" Jill sat back and gave Jase and Lainey the same once-over. "Maybe you two would like to tell us what you've been up to since the shop closed. Perhaps making hot and spicy…" She paused long enough to make Jase squirm and wonder what she was about to say. "…spaghetti, because this is *not* Batallio's and the pasta is downright soggy." Jill looked into Jase's eyes and he knew that she was completely aware of exactly what was going on.

Lainey giggled at his side. "Caught. And I was going to use the ever-so-believable *'we were just hangin' out and stuff'* excuse." Lainey studied Henry who still fidgeted.

Jill pushed her chair back. "Good one, always a reliable explanation. But the difference is we were really just hanging out, not cookin'." Her expressive eyes, much like her mother's, widened for a moment. "Thanks for supper, *Jase*. Come on, Henry, we should check the school site and see if our history teacher has posted any homework assignments."

"I know old Westlake is a ball breaker, right?" Henry said, picking up his plate and following Jill, who seemed eager to get away.

Jason threw his arm over the back of Lainey's chair. "It would seem we have fooled no one."

Lainey shrugged. "Maybe it's better this way. It's all out in the open. This way Jilly can get used to things being different. And so can I. And you can get used to me having a kid. I get the impression you haven't dated many women with kids."

"Is it that obvious?"

"Mmm, you just have to get used to being second, for a little while. Jill comes first. I'll tell you that right now."

"Oh, *I* got that. And it shouldn't be any other way. I'm a big boy, I can take it."

"I know you're a big boy." She bit her lip. Her eyes turned warm as she twisted in her chair, facing him.

"Why Ms Clarkson, I'm beginning to think you are insatiable."

"Is that a problem?" she asked insinuating herself between his knees. He opened his legs wider to allow her closer. She stared at his lips waiting for an answer.

"Problem? No, that's definitely not a problem," he said as she wound her arms around his neck. Aggressively, she kissed him until the kids squabbling in the next room made her come up for air.

"Time and privacy seem to be the predicament," Jason said, smoothing his hand over her back.

Lainey took a deep cleansing breath. "So crawling into your lap right now is probably not a good idea?" she purred.

An impatient noise escaped him. "It's a fantastic idea. Let's go back to my place and I'll just let you have your way with me."

Lainey made a humming sound in her throat as if she might've liked that idea.

"Hey, Mom?" Jill's voice cut into their banter.

Sighing reluctantly, Lainey moved away from Jason, putting an appropriate amount of space between them. "Yes, Jilly?"

"You heard from Dad in the last couple days?"

Lainey harrumphed. "No."

Jill poked her head into the room. "I've sent him several different texts for three consecutive days and nothing. He always answers my texts."

Lainey shook her head. "Who knows, Jill? Maybe he lost his phone. Perhaps he broke it. Have you tried shooting him an email or you could just call him if you're worried about him."

"I'm not worried. It's just weird." She slipped back into the other room with Henry.

Lainey got up and started clearing the plates. Jason stood and helped, carrying the empty containers to the garbage.

"She's worried," Lainey said.

"Or she just wanted to bring up her dad in front of me," Jason hedged.

"You think?" Lainey's nose crinkled prettily.

He shrugged. "She kinda laid it on the line for me while you were on the phone."

"She did?"

"Yeah."

"I'm sorry. Are you mad?"

"Of course not. She loves you. She doesn't want some joker coming in here and hurting her mother."

"Are you a joker?" Her question was teasing but her eyes were not. He knew that she was asking that instead of going right to the hurting part.

"I told you I'm a teacher, not a comedian." Everyone was worried about Lainey, which he understood. But he was getting a little concerned about himself. What if he was the one to get hurt here? He'd never felt this way about any woman. And it had happened so fast, so instantaneously for him. From the moment he'd met her he'd wanted to know more. And now that he knew more, he wanted it all. She had him thinking about things that he'd never given a second thought to. Like marriage and kids. Like forever.

"I can see that. You're looking very serious right now. I'm going to ask you the most hated question that a woman can ask a man. What are you thinking?"

"Eww, sharing feelings. I think I wanna shudder."

Lainey waited.

"Do you keep in touch with your husband?"

"No. We only talk about Jill if I have to speak to him at all. Or whatever lawsuit or papers he's had drawn up. Yeah, so mostly through our lawyers and through Jill."

Lainey piled the dishes into the sink and started the hot water, pouring some dish soap around in a big circle.

"You were with him a long time. Right out of high school? Got the old twenty-two on the ankle."

"We got married right after high school and then I got

pregnant with Jilly."

"Is that what you told people?"

She blinked up at him.

"I'm willing to bet you walked out of that high school with a diploma in one hand and Jill already growing inside you, *then* got married." A slight nod confirmed it. Jason leaned against the sink. "Wow. You've never been with anyone else, have you?" Not even the cop that her ex had accused her of sleeping with.

Lainey shut off the water and gazed out of the window into the darkness. "Not until a few hours ago, no, I've never been with anybody else," she said quietly.

Jason inhaled deeply and exhaled heavily. *Well fuck!* How the hell was he supposed to compete with that? Thad was her first love and lover, father of her child, a marriage, a whole fucking lifetime together. Jase should just face it now. He was the rebound guy. He was doomed.

Lainey laid a hand on his stomach and neared him. "Is that a problem? I thought guys liked it when a girl wasn't well used. You seem appalled by that fact that I've only been with one man."

Jason folded his arms around her back and pulled her even closer. "No, that's not it at all."

Her face fell. "Was I not good?" Her gaze darted around his face.

"Come on, you were there, do you honestly have to ask me that? You were fantastic. You are fantastic. We were fantastic together. I wanna do it again right now."

Her face lightened then pinkened. "Then what is it?"

"I just don't know how I'm supposed to compete with what you had with him? You had a whole lifetime with the guy."

Lainey was so shocked. Jason seemed like the most confident man in the world, but he was worried that he couldn't compete with history. "You're right. We had a lifetime. And he killed it. The only good thing left of our union is Jilly. There is nothing left but sad memories. Besides it's not a competition. We're just getting to know each other, right? Making some new memories." And strangely enough, remembering Thad didn't seem to hurt as much with Jason standing there.

"Getting to know each other? You don't have sex with just anybody, Lainey."

"That's my daughter talking."

"And me, too. You just said yourself you've never been with anybody else. That's a lot for a guy to have to live up to. You're expecting this to go somewhere."

Lainey lowered her gaze. Her face and ears grew hot, waiting for the brush-off to come, when she felt his finger under her chin lifting, forcing her to face him. "I want this to go somewhere too," he acknowledged.

"You do?" she breathed as her heart raced. His dark eyes searched hers before he lowered his head taking her lips. This was a sweet kiss, not the hungry all-consuming combustible kind of kiss they usually shared, but all the more potent with the sentiment and emotion behind it.

Jason ended the kiss. She stared up at him and his insides melted. *Fuck! I'm falling in love with her. What the fuck? How do I stop myself from doing this?*

He had to tell her the truth. Before someone else did. Or, worse, she found out on the Internet or from some magazine.

"You two are worse than teenagers, Dub." Henry sauntered into the kitchen like it was his own. "You gonna stand there all night and look at her or are you gonna kiss her already. Geez, J-Dub, have I taught you nothing?" Henry reached into the fridge and took another soda.

Jason never took his eyes off Lainey. "I'm waiting for her to kiss me. Remember? She promised."

"Go for it, Ms C, or he'll never teach another class without stumbling over his own tongue for an hour and a half. It's torture."

Henry vacated the room but she didn't kiss him. "What are you waiting for?" Jason asked.

Slowly she raked her teeth across her full bottom lip. "I'm afraid if I start kissing you now, I'll never stop."

His eyes almost crossed. Jason pulled her against him. "I wanna take you home."

Her arms tightened around him. "That sounds perfect."

But their night wouldn't end the way either of them wanted. He took a deep breath. "Let's get these dishes done and I'll go home."

"Don't worry about it. I'll take care of them. But you don't have to go."

"I need to go. Or I will not be held responsible for my actions."

She made a choking sound. "Then I'll walk you out."

"G'night, Jill, Henry," Jason called.

"G'night, J-Dub."

"Goodnight, Mister Westlake," Jill retorted, coolly.

Jason held Lainey's hand as she walked him to his Porsche. Jason leaned against it and pulled her into his arms. "Christ, I haven't had to say goodnight like this in… I don't know how long."

"Maybe next week, when Jill goes to see her father, we can spend the whole weekend together?"

"Was that a question?" he asked, sardonically. "Hell yeah!" He kissed her goodnight until his heart raced and he had another raging hard-on. She clung to him until finally he set her away from him and got into the car. "I will see you tomorrow."

Jason decided on his way home, he'd tell her the truth on their weekend alone.

Chapter Eleven

At lunchtime the next day at school, Jason checked his phone for messages hoping there would be one from Lainey. When he saw her name on the screen, his stomach jolted and he had to smile at his own weakness for this woman.

"Can you meet me for lunch?" he read out loud.

Ah, hell yeah, he texted back.

Almost immediately a response popped up. *Meet me at your place in ten?*

I'm there, he wrote and hightailed it out of the school.

Lainey was already there waiting patiently in the driveway when he pulled up. God she looked beautiful. How did she just keep getting better and better-looking? Today she wore a classy double-breasted navy dress with gold buttons, almost military style, her dark hair done in a loose knot. He wanted to get his fingers into it.

Jason unfolded his tall frame from the little sports car. "Hey, beautiful." Snagging her around the waist, he pulled her to him before taking her lips in a long hot kiss.

When he finally came up for air she breathed, "Well, hello, handsome. I think you just squished our sandwiches."

He shrugged. "That's okay."

They walked up to the front door and he unlocked it. The minute they were inside and the door shut, she was back in his arms, kissing him madly. He was just about to tackle the buttons down the front of her dress when she started to sink down in front of him. Unfastening the button and fly of his tailored pants, she had them open before he could blink. Impatiently, she worked them over his hips and released his swollen cock to the air.

"God, Lainey, what are you doing to me?"

"Shh, I've been thinking about this all morning," she confessed as she licked her lips, then slid them, warm and firm, around the head.

She pushed him back against the door.

Fuck! She'd been thinking about *this* all morning? She'd been thinking of giving him head? Thinking about his dick? Sucking it? His thoughts as well as what she was doing to him were going to make him come way too soon for his liking.

Jason splayed his fingers into her hair, holding her head as she ran her tongue from the bulbous head to the root, stopping to suck each ball softly, one by one, before making the journey back up. Jason watched it all from above. Her eyes were closed as if she were enjoying it too, maybe savoring it as much as he was. Having the visual along with the sensation was almost more than he could take.

Lainey licked the pre-cum from the tip before taking the crown into her mouth again. She made a humming sound of appreciation in the back of her throat, causing him to moan in response. She pulled his cock forward and took as much as she could, letting her lips and jaw close firmly around him, replicating her hot wet cunt. He closed his eyes and opened his mouth, breathing hard.

Lainey wrapped her hand around the base of his dick as she withdrew back up to the tip. Then she began to go down on him until the tip hit the back of her throat. While making a fist she attempted to make up the rest of the distance. She began to pump her hand in conjunction with the mouth action.

Jason's heart pounded, along with his blood. His grip tightened in her hair as he moaned his pleasure loudly. "Ahh, fuck, Lainey!" He gritted his teeth as she picked up the tempo even more.

Jason felt the hot rush of excitement building and building, higher and faster as she expertly sucked and stoked his eager cock. He clamped down on his glutes and tightened his thighs trying to stave off the inevitable, to eke out one more second of pleasure. But when she closed her other hand around his balls and she reached with her fingers adding some pressure back there, it was all over for him.

"Aww, God!" he hissed, dragging his hands out of her hair, placing them to her cheeks, stroking her in appreciation as he sprayed the back of her throat.

"Mmm," she hummed again, not letting up on the rhythm until she'd milked every last drop from him. When she finally released her hold, he pulled her head against his stomach just hugging her.

She moved her hands up to his hips.

"Mmm," Jason repeated. "Whoa!"

With her eyes half closed in desire, she looked up at him, her face flushed, her lips pink and swollen and she smiled at him.

He would never forget her expression. "You thought about *that* all morning?" he asked, his voice raspy.

She kissed his stomach and he helped her to her feet. "Yes," she said simply, rising. "I can't seem to keep you out of my mind either."

"And you thought about *that*? Fuck me, how could I be so lucky?"

She grinned. "Ya liked that, huh?"

"Liked? Liked is too tame a word for that."

Jason pulled her against him and he felt her tremble. He may have been lucky but she was still suffering some major arousal, he guessed. He started to pull up the skirt of her form-fitting dress. She resisted at first. "What are you doing?" she said attempting to smooth the material back down.

"Let me touch you."

"No."

"Come on, let me touch you. I know you're turned on."
She smirked and blushed.

They waged a tug of war for a moment before he decided to try a different tactic. He kissed her, hotly, teasing her until finally she worked her hands around his neck, and he seized the opportunity to pull her skirt up to her waist. There was no fight left in her.

Jason eased his palm down into her panties, allowing his fingers to sweep between her lips. He was met with soft, hot, slick liquid just waiting to be savored.

"Now what I wanna know is," he whispered into her mouth, "were you this wet from thinking about what you were going to do to me, or was it doing it to me that got you so worked up?"

She didn't answer, just kept kissing him hotly.

As soon as his fingers grazed her wet pussy, her mouth opened on his, in a quick inhalation of suspended pleasure and he knew by her response that she was on the very edge of an orgasm. He was torn. He wanted to sink down to his knees and return the favor, but he also wanted to take his time, the first time he licked her, to get her to this kind of peak. He wanted to taste her in every stage of arousal, from timid beginning to this beautiful slick end and everything in between. To hear the little noises she made when he did something she liked. To feel her excitement grow and expand until she convulsed and undulated under the assault of his tongue gliding through her folds and his lips sucking her to climax.

Running all four fingers into her crease from back to front he'd have to settle for fingering her for now. She seemed to melt at his touch. He paused to circle slowly and deliberately the hot hole begging to have something long and hard buried in it. She gasped when he slid his middle digit into her. But he didn't stay sheathed for long before he swirled it over the tiny engorged bud burning for his touch.

Lainey exhaled in a rush. She wasn't even kissing him anymore, she'd leaned her head into his shoulder, clinging to him as he stroked her with tiny slow circles. A small whimper escaped her lips right before she shuddered against him. He continued the little rounds until she flattened her hand over his so that he cupped her pussy. She needed the added pressure, he assumed.

"Feel better?" he asked, when she calmed. He knew he didn't. He was now back where they started with another intense boner.

"No," she said breathlessly. "I want it all," she admitted, palming his erection.

He groaned, thrusting his hips, making sure she felt the fullness.

She glanced at her watch. "But you, Professor, need to get back to school. I hear they frown on the teachers being late."

"I seriously don't know how you expect me to go back there. I am indecent, just like you had me at the park. My mind will be here," he indicated where she'd been kneeling in front of him just moments before. "I won't be able to speak. And I'll be thinking about this," he gave her box a squeeze, "and your sweet freakin' mouth the whole fuckin' time."

Tilting her pelvis she then pushed her sweet cunt more fully into his hand before she stepped away and shimmied her tight skirt back down over her delicious ass. "Would you like me to apologize then? Take it back? Never ask you if you're free for lunch ever again?"

"No," he answered sulkily.

"Then do up your pants like a good boy and let's go."

He did, tucking his disobedient cock back into his pants, zipping up with a grimace and a tug to readjust.

They walked back out into the sunshine. Jason locked the door and followed Lainey down the drive to her car.

"Here, eat this on your way back." She handed him a sandwich.

"Thanks."

"I meant to make you happy, not sullen." She pouted.

"I am. You did." He sighed heavily and pulled her into his embrace. "I just want you so fuckin' bad, all the time."

"Me too."

"I just want to curl up and take our time. We are always in a rush."

"I know we are. But next weekend we can take our time," she said into his chest.

It seemed like an eternity. He eased back so that he could look at her but still keep her in his arms. "I can't wait. I want to go to sleep buried inside you and wake up with you in my arms."

When her eyes softened, his heart stuttered. "That sounds wonderful," she breathed.

He kissed her softly then let her go. She got into her car. With his car parked behind, he had to back out first. He pulled out and reversed far enough back so that she could get out and he followed her until they had to go their separate ways. As he drove level she gave him a wave and a smile. He nodded as he turned in the other direction.

****

Jason opened the door of the shop at exactly four p.m. Lainey looked up at his abrupt entrance and smiled. "Hey, handsome."

"Are you alone?" he asked, in a clipped tone.

"Yes," she answered, her smile fading.

"Get in the back room. Now!" he said, in a low authoritative voice. She hesitated but when he turned the 'Open' sign to 'Closed' and locked the door, she started to back into the little room. In large strides he followed, stalking her, loosening his tie as he came at her.

She was almost to the back wall when his large body shadowed the doorframe.

Lainey watched him warily. He seemed almost angry. Intense.

"Any cameras back here?"

She shook her head.

Locking the back door he then moved like a caged cat to where she stood.

Without a word he dragged her skirt up. His jaw was tight, like he had his teeth clamped tightly together. His lips were drawn in a hard line. Once he had her skirt up around her waist, he tucked the index fingers under the soft elastic in her panties and as he started to kneel down in front of her, he dragged the garment to her ankles on his descent.

Lainey's pussy pooled with weighty desire when she knew his intent. His teeth grazed the skin hooding her clit. She closed her eyes and leaned heavily against the wall. He ran his tongue lightly over her smooth lips, as far back between her thighs as he could reach, then back to the front. Lainey tensed in anticipation, wanting, needing him to touch his tongue to the burning nub. But he teased her, running it to the other side and back.

Lainey fisted her hands in frustration. The flat of Jason's tongue tapped tantalizingly close to the highly sensitized bud.

Gasping for breath, she knew she wasn't even going to get to enjoy this. Jason had her in such a heightened state of semi-permanent arousal all the time that she knew just a few velvety strokes on her highly sensitized clit would have her in one big wet puddle in no time.

Lainey tensed every muscle she could think of trying to slow the incredible feeling building inside her.

He grabbed her by the hips, pulling her forward. "Open," he growled, releasing his hold only to coax her thighs further apart. "Do you think I've been able to keep my mind anywhere else?" he asked, staring at her crotch, his heavy breath sending hot gusts of air across her thighs. "I've thought of two things all afternoon, thanks to you. I thought about lunchtime, and how you sucked my cock." Another harsh sound erupted from his throat and he nipped at her skin, making Lainey cry out but not in pain. "Ah, fuck, did you suck my cock! And then I couldn't wait to return the favor. I could think of nothing but slipping my tongue into you, tasting you for the first time."

Lainey couldn't help the pathetic mewling sound from escaping her throat.

With his thumbs, he opened her lips and licked in one long searing stroke from her hot wet hole to her swollen nub. They both sighed in ecstasy.

Jason sucked her clit gently into his mouth, probing softly. Her legs trembled.

"Oh, Jase," she cried softly, shuddering into a quick but deep orgasm.

"Ahh, already?" he complained, without heat.

"I'm sorry, you just do it for me."

He grinned at that admission, rising to his feet. She looked up at him with soft satisfied eyes. "Did you bring a condom?" she asked hopefully.

He raised a dark eyebrow at her. "As a matter of fact…" He reached into his back pocket and produced a foil packet. "I did."

"Oh, good," she breathed and eagerly went after the button and zipper of his trousers. She pushed them off his hips, along with his boxers, sending them in one fell swoop down to his ankles, while he tore open the packet. Lainey took his quivering cock into her hands and stroked him. When he placed the rubber over the tip she rolled it the rest of the way down.

"Sit," she instructed, indicating the padded chair to their left. He sat his bare ass onto the cool leather. Lainey backed toward him. Jason placed a hand on her hip as he held his cock straight up and steady. The tip nudged into her hot center. She eased slowly down, inch by delicious inch. When the backs of her thighs touched his, Jason grabbed her hips and yanked her down hard into his lap, impaling her completely. He growled deep in his throat at the sensation of her sitting on him. He held her there for a moment, savoring, then she started to move, using the arms of the chair as leverage. Slowly at first, in an up and down rhythm, using him as if she were rubbing some sweet spot inside herself, trying to soothe an itch. He let her set the pace. She could use him for whatever reason she needed. She felt incredible to him. Hot and tight.

He reached around her, taking her soft tits in his hands. He gave them a squeeze before stroking her nipples to twin peaks. She exhaled heavily and arched into his hold. He made circular motions in tandem. The little noises she made drove him crazy. He felt the tiniest little flutter deep inside her. Her breathing escalated and she picked up the tempo.

Another convulsion made her muscles clench around his throbbing hardness. Everything inside him quickened, his pulse, his blood, his need to fuck her senseless. Releasing her breasts he then grabbed her hips and slammed her down onto his thighs.

She emitted a strangled scream. He froze for a moment thinking he'd been too rough. When she surged upward, gritting, "Go! Faster!"

He wasn't content to just sit in the chair anymore. He bucked, jolting her to her feet. He followed her up, keeping as much of himself embedded in her as he could. Sliding his palms down her arms he placed her hands on the worktable in front of them. He bent her forward, his chest to her back. "Hold on, my Lainey love," he whispered in warning.

Jason took control and she was glad. He rubbed his thick hardness back and forth, sliding in and almost all the way out of her. Climax building with each thrust. Raspy cries of pleasure erupted from her parched throat every time he plunged forward. He dropped his hips and began to move up and into her in a circular motion. The sweet undulation began from a spot deep inside her and radiated out encompassing him surging behind her. Lainey moaned.

"Oh, yeah," Jason wheezed in appreciation as he felt the delicate little flutters get stronger, clenching around him, driving him to his own massive explosion.

They stayed in the position as they struggled to recover

their breath. Lainey was the first to move. She straightened from her bent position, and wrapped her arms backward around his neck. He encircled her waist.

"Wow, Mr Westlake, you really know how to…make an…entrance."

He snorted, his cock jerked inside her and she trembled with latent desire.

"You are seriously driving me crazy, woman. I can't even do my job. I've resorted to assigning all four classes with chapter after chapter of silent reading because I can't seem so speak anymore without making some kind of sexual innuendo or naming some female body part."

Lainey giggled, thinking he was kidding.

"And let me tell you, you have some fine body parts," he said as she turned in his arms to face him. He wrapped his hands around her bare ass, holding her firmly against him. "And on our weekend, I intend to worship every one of them."

"I can't wait." Standing on her tiptoes she gently kissed his chin. "I guess I should open the store back up."

"Oh, Geez, yeah. Shit. Sorry. I wasn't thinking," he stammered in apology.

"Not like it really matters," she said with a sigh. Grudgingly, she released him and shimmied her dress back down. "I'll be right back," she said collecting her undergarments and disappearing into the bathroom.

Jason had readjusted his own clothes by the time she reappeared.

"You look like you haven't been ravished, Mr Westlake," she grinned, jerking on his tie.

"I haven't, Ms Clarkson, I believe I was the one doing the ravishing."

"And a fine job you did," she said, leaving their little room. He followed as she went to the door and unlocked it, turning the sign back around to 'Open'.

"Only fifteen more minutes anyway, Lainey."

"Yep, fifteen minutes and by the end of next week that

'Closed' sign just might be permanent."

"Oh?" Jason asked frowning. "Did something else happen?" He didn't know many details about the litigation concerning the shop or the house for that matter. They'd never really talked about it. The only information he had were little bits Lainey had dropped, what Henry had confided and the crap he'd read on the unreliable Internet.

With a wave of her hand she indicated a thick envelope sitting by the register. "Thad happened."

Jason reached for the envelope then hesitated, waiting for permission. The last thing he wanted to do right now was overstep the boundaries.

"Go 'head."

Picking up the paperwork, he then began to scan the legal jargon.

"He wants you to buy him outright? Pay all the legal fees and pay off all the vendors who have also filed suit. And any other fees that may occur…"

"Blah, blah, blah. The long and the short of it is I don't have it and he knows it. And even if the house sells, it won't sell in time for me to do anything but shut the damn doors and then I am still on the hook for everything that is owed."

"Why is he doing this?" Jason asked, not understanding.

"Because he can."

"Lainey, who the hell is your lawyer?"

She looked at him, confused.

"I mean, I realize this is none of my business and I have only a vague idea of what caused your divorce, but any half decent lawyer would pull this apart in no time. Thad's just pushing you around."

She nodded. "Also, because he can. He's the one with the million dollar signing. He has the money to hire the kind of lawyers who can chew mine apart. Actually, the lawyer we've had all along has been a friend of ours from school, Reg Pool, but when Thad made it big, he dropped both of us."

"Your lawyer is a friend?"

"Reg is a good lawyer, Jason, he's just small town good, not corporate conglomerate good."

"Is this small town good barrister going after Thad for future earnings?"

Vaguely, she shook her head.

"You were with Thad when he wasn't famous. You probably supported him and Jill while he ran off to training camps and stuff, right? You are entitled to his future prospects too, Lainey. You helped him get there. He owes you that. And you said something about him in talks with other teams? You can get in on that too. Or endorsement deals?"

"No. I don't want anything from him anymore. I just want out. I want to sever all ties with him. But I feel like I will never be able to do that because of Jilly. I am always going to have to deal with him in some way or another."

"So you're just going to let him take everything from you? If he wants to fight dirty, we can too."

Her gaze darted all around Jason's face. "We?" she asked weakly.

"Yeah, we," he answered, supportively. He wasn't going anywhere. And if Thad wanted to throw his money around, Jason could match him, meet him and bury him in it.

"That's really sweet of you to offer and all, but it's practically over. And maybe it's for the best. A new start all around is just what Jill and I need. A new job, a new house without the memories and perhaps even a new place. I don't know where we're going to end up. I just might follow Jill when she leaves for college." She shrugged. "Who knows?"

Jason wasn't about to get into that one right now. One step at a time here. Everything between them was happening so fast. He needed to take a step back for a minute. But he knew that he didn't want her moving away.

He was deep in thought, dragging on his lower lip when she approached him. "Hey, this is my problem. Don't worry about it. Okay?" She took his hand away from his mouth. He gave her a quick nod but knew that he was going to be giving his lawyer a call before the night ended.

Lainey closed up the register. Jason stuffed the paperwork into his suit coat pocket while she was distracted.

"Did you have any customers today?"

"No."

"Do you even like this, Lainey? Is this shop even worth fighting for? You don't seem like your heart is even in it?"

"I don't know anymore. It was fun for me in the beginning. It gave me something to do when he was out of town all the time and Jilly was in school full-time. But now it's just something else that he ruined for me, you know? It was something of my own and now he claims it was all his."

"Then change it up. Get some new and different things in here. Something that every other boutique on the block doesn't have. You'll bring in new people."

"And what would that be?"

They don't have Jase West, he thought briefly, then discarded that idea. Another thing he had to deal with. Lainey wasn't even aware that she had Jase West at her disposal. And he was sure that was only a matter of time. And in the end, wasn't that what Thad had done? Shown up on opening day lending his name and his celebrity to get the press then never came back.

"So, what are your plans for tonight?" Lainey asked.

"Um, I don't know. Do you need to get home?"

"No, Jill's with Henry again."

"Then let's go to my place," he suggested, following her out of the door. He took the key from her and locked it.

"I should go home…and shower."

"I have a shower at my house. Follow me." He didn't give her a chance to refuse but stalked off across the street to his Porsche.

* * * *

And a fine shower he had. Just like everything else in Jason's house, the shower was massive and open, built for two or more. They'd barely made it in the door when he picked her up and ran up the stairs with her. They'd shared a very hot and steamy, soapy and slippery shower that had ended in another fabulous orgasm.

Lainey sat at Jason's kitchen island in one of his T-shirts, her hair damp, watching him putter around making supper.

"What are you thinking about?" Jason asked, as he threw two steaks onto the grill.

"Mmm," she stretched. "I was thinking about the shower."

He grinned. "I could turn these babies off and we could go for another one," he said leaning across the counter and laying a kiss on the end of her nose. "You feel good all slippery and wet."

"Ditto!" She leaned into him and kissed him thoroughly. "The steaks, Jase."

"Oh shit!" He rushed back to the grill, sticking in a fork to turn the meat over. "Jesus, woman, the day that I can— Ouch!" he yelped as he singed the end of his finger. "Fuck! The day I can do menial freakin' tasks again without falling on my ass, blurting something inappropriate in front of my students or burning myself, I will be a happy man."

"But I won't be," she sulked. "That will mean that we've lost our magic."

He worked his way back over and took her face into his hands. "No, it won't. By then the magic will be even better."

"Do you think so? I like this. I like feeling this way. Everything is so new and perfect. I can't wait to see you or hear your voice or simply get a text. I like learning all these new things about you. It's exciting."

The soft way she was looking at him while she spoke made his heart pound so loud that he could hear it in his own ears.

"I don't want all that to go away," she continued. "Ever. I like that maybe I might have the same effect on you as you do on me. I always want to feel for you what I feel right now."

What was she saying?

"What are you feeling?" he asked.

"The steaks," she reminded, avoiding the question.

"What?"

"You need to take the steaks off, they're burning."

Turning, he took the steaks off and tossed them on a plate. "Maybe you should cook until I can control myself."

She laughed and hopped off the stool. Coming around the counter, she encircled his waist. "You're just lucky I don't mind mine well done."

They sat down and ate steak and tossed salad.

Just as they were finishing up the phone rang. Jason reached to grab it. "Talk ta me. Oh, hey, Mom. No, it's always a good time."

Lainey disappeared while he talked to his mother and when she came back to his disappointment she was dressed.

"I'm gonna go," Lainey whispered, thumbing toward the door.

"No wait...Lainey..." Jason said. "Just a sec, Mom," he said into the phone before setting it down.

"You don't have to go," he appealed, pulling Lainey into his arms when he caught up to her by the door.

"Yeah, I do. I should get home before Jill does," she responded, tucking her head under his chin and holding him close.

"And you said yourself that you've been neglecting your work because of me. So I'll get out of your way and you can do some work. I'll see you tomorrow?" she asked hopefully, looking up at him.

He chuckled. She still didn't get how into her he was. "Try to keep me away," he said before he took her lips.

He remained at the door until she drove down the street before he went back to the phone.

"Hey, Ma, sorry, I'm back now."

"Who is Lainey, son?"

"Oh, Ma, who is Lainey? Now that's a question and a half."

"*Oh?*" She sounded too interested.

"Ma, you're not going to believe this but I think she's the one." There. He'd said it. Not only out loud but to another person—his mom no less. It was real and it was out there. "Mom? Mom? You still there?"

"I'm still here, Jase, I just can't believe what I just heard. You think she's the one? Why is it this is the first that we've heard about her? Have you been keeping her a secret?"

"No. It's a really new thing. I just met her last week—"

"Last week! You met her last week and you're telling me she's the one. You mean she's the one *this* week. Let's get it straight, Jason. Another one will catch your interest and you'll be off chasing the next *one*. How could you do that to me? Get my hopes up for nothing."

"It's not like that. I've never felt like this before. I don't even wanna look at other women right now. She's all I can think about. I can't even teach for fuck's sake—"

"Jason!"

"Sorry, Mom. I can't teach. I wanna be with her all the time."

"Hmmm. That does sound different. For you, at least. So tell me about her. Her name is Lainey and what else?"

"She's gorgeous. She owns a boutique downtown. She's beautiful. She's a mom—"

"She has a child? Oh, Jason, she's a gold digger—"

"Don't ever say that again!" he yelled, thinking of the headlines that he'd seen on the Internet. He tried to soften it with, "She doesn't even know who I am. So you can get that out of your head right now. Her daughter is a student of mine. That's how we met. Last week during parent-teacher interviews."

"Oh, she's not even a little child. I was thinking a toddler. Huh. That's different."

"Yeah. I told you this was."

"So, how is it she doesn't know who you are? I thought that you had that speech with your students on your first day?"

"I did, but her daughter didn't tell her about it. Apparently she wasn't impressed in the least."

"You are getting older, son. You can't keep the teeny boppers on the hook forever."

"Thanks, Mom."

"No problem. Who can keep you more humble than your mother? Now, I still don't understand how she's never heard of you or seen you—you were all over the tabloids and the news, especially when they were hounding you about quitting the music biz."

"That's a long story."

"I have time."

"Yeah, well I don't. We'll get into that another time. Now I need a favor…"

Chapter Twelve

Lainey sat behind the counter, watching traffic go by outside the shop. She'd already decided to start packing up the surplus in the back. It was paid for. If she could sell it off, maybe she could pay somebody. Or maybe she could send it back. She wouldn't get full cost refunded if she returned it but at least it would be less she owed.

It had been a crappy morning. Her lawyer's secretary had called first thing and informed her that Reg had taken a leave of absence suddenly and would have to put off all of his cases until he got back. He'd be placing Lainey's caseload with a colleague. Lainey asked the assistant when she could expect to hear from Reg's associate and that didn't sound promising either. Now there was no way that she could fight Thad without Reg's help, especially with the next deadline being next Friday.

A large streaming shadow crossed the window out front. Lainey sat up straight as the bell on the door chimed and a group of women trailed into the shop. They weren't her usual clientele.

"Good morning," Lainey greeted, standing. All five ladies turned and looked at her, giving her the once-over.

"Oh, lovely," said one.

"Yes, indeed," agreed another in a whisper.

"I told you," one sniffed.

"Can I help you?" Lainey asked, a little confused by the comments.

"You have a lovely little place here. We were driving by and just had to stop."

"Oh, that's wonderful," Lainey beamed. "Come in. Have

a look around. If you need any help just let me know." Lainey didn't like to hover over the customers.

"And your name is, Miss?" One severe-looking woman rapped out like a drill sergeant.

"I'm Lainey."

"Right. Lainey, girls. Lainey."

"Is that short for something? Say Elaine or Elena?"

"No, just Lainey."

There was another round of whispered commentary.

They were a whirlwind. Picking things up, asking questions, placing things on the counter. One lady went as far as to take a picture of a dress with her cellphone and send it to her granddaughter to see if she would like it. When the answer was yes, she placed it on the counter as well.

It was almost noon by the time Lainey had them all cashed out, packed up and bagged.

"Well, this was wonderful, Lainey. I am going to recommend you to everyone I know between here and Jacksonville."

"I've already tweeted about it," the same woman who'd bought the dress for her granddaughter said.

"Why, thank you, that's very nice of you. But I'm not sure how long I'll be open."

"What!" came joint outrage.

"I'm having a bit of legal trouble and, well, I won't get into details but it's not looking good."

"My son's a lawyer, sweetie." The severe-looking woman handed Lainey a card.

Lainey took it politely and looked down at it, stunned.

"You give him a call. He'll take care of you."

"And he's single," another chimed, but received an elbow for it from one of the other ladies, who watched Lainey carefully.

Lainey smiled at her.

"Are you married?" the lady who had given the elbow asked.

"No. Divorced. Well, almost."

"Do you have kids?"

"Yes, a teenage daughter."

"Are you seeing anyone?" another asked.

"Yes," Lainey smiled and bit her lip. It was the first time she'd been asked that question since Jason had come into her life and it felt good to say that she was with someone. "I'm seeing someone."

"Someone special then?" They must have picked up on her feelings.

"Yes, someone very special." Lainey almost felt teary. Getting a lump in her throat. He'd become so important to her so quickly. She liked Jason so much. However she wasn't ready to define what she was feeling. But whatever it was, it felt wonderful. She made eye contact with the elbow lady again and she nodded as if she approved. Lainey thought that was strange.

"Well, we need to get going. We're meeting my son for lunch." Again it was the elbow lady that spoke. There was something very familiar about her.

In a line, they trooped out of the door. "Thank you for stopping in," Lainey called.

"I'm sure we'll be seeing you again, dear."

Lainey watched them get into two separate cars and they waved to her as they pulled away.

It had gone from such a shitty day to a good day. They'd lifted her spirits and put some much needed cash into the register.

And if Jason could meet her for lunch, the day would be awesome. Lainey shot Jason a text and while she waited for a reply, she read the card that the nice lady had left for her. 'Cam Bowman, Attorney to the Starz'. She'd never be able to afford someone like that.

She set it down to answer her ringing cell. "Hello?"

"Hey, baby, sorry, I'm tied up for lunch today. Can I meet you after work?"

"Oh." She was disappointed. She wanted to see him.

"Sure. I wasn't certain what your schedule was like. I'll see you later then."

"Lainey?"

"Yeah?"

"You okay?"

"Yeah, it's been an up and down morning. I'll tell you all about it later. Have a good afternoon."

"You too, Lainey love."

She stared at the phone as she set it back down on the counter. It wasn't the first time he'd called her that. But usually it was during an intimate moment. Did he realize he was saying it? Did he even mean it or was it just a pet thing, like when he called her beautiful or baby?

Lainey spent the rest of the afternoon floating around in a fog of new feelings. Even though she might lose the shop she didn't let it get to her. Doing some research she got on the net and looked up 'Cam Bowman, Attorney to the Starz'. So when the phone rang and the man on the other end introduced himself as Cam Bowman, Lainey was taken off guard. When he asked for her by name she panicked and told him that Lainey wasn't in. He left a number where he could be reached and gave specific instructions that he needed to hear back from her by the end of the business day.

After making herself a steaming hot cup of tea, she gathered her courage and made the call.

Cam Bowman was brisk and straightforward — a take the bull by the horns kind of guy.

As soon as he came on the line, he took charge.

"Mrs Markham, I'm glad you called. I've been looking over the records to your shop, gone through the court proceedings thus far, in accordance to your pending divorce and had a good laugh at your husband's attempt to screw you — excuse my language — out of your business, your home and custody of one minor child, uhh, Jillian, I see here."

"And how is it that you have access to that information,

Mr Bowman? Neither Thad or I are a client of yours." Lainey trod lightly.

"It's all public knowledge, Mrs Markham."

"I go by Clarkson now."

"Yes, I believe I read that also. Forgive the oversight. Now, I am going to fax some documents over that will need your signature. Just a quick formality showing that I have taken you on as a client. I will also have some other forms for you to sign. I'll have those couriered."

"Other forms?"

"Yes, I have some backers. Clients with cash willing to pour lots and lots of capital into your store. You can pay your creditors..."

"Wait. Hold on a minute. This is all going too fast. I haven't even agreed to your representation, Mr Bowman."

"Agreed? What is there to think about? Ms Clarkson, I can have your husband on his knees by this time tomorrow. Just give me the go-ahead and it's all but done."

"Although that sounds very tempting, Mr Bowman, I'm not sure that I want to sink down to his level. And about these backers? Who are they and what do they want from me? What's in it for them? The shop isn't even turning a profit. Why on earth would anyone want to buy into this mess?"

"I know this must seem a little overwhelming for you. But this is all on the up and up. I am an extremely capable attorney, Ms Clarkson, and I would never steer a client into a shady deal. Once you've read over the proposal, I'm certain you'll have no misgivings. Their offer is more than generous and they've agreed to be silent partners, in addition to providing the funds necessary to pay off your creditors as well as pump some much needed cash into your shop. But I'll need to deal with Mr Markham first. What do you say, Ms Clarkson, Lainey, will you accept me as your representation?"

"I cannot afford to pay you, Mr Bowman."

"Can you afford a dollar?"

"Well, yes, of course, but…"

"Then we have a deal, Lainey. I am now your lawyer."

"But why? I don't understand."

"I will take a percentage of whatever settlement we reach with Mr Markham. This is kind of a high profile case. I'm actually surprised that someone hasn't snatched you up already."

"Oh. You want the press, is that it, Mr Bowman? Well, you can forget it. The press hates me and the sentiment is mutual. I will not sell my morals to you so that you can make more of a name for yourself. By what I read, you don't need a small time case like mine anyway. That would just be a step down for you."

"We'll play this however you like, Lainey. I am at your disposal. I work for you. You call the shots. I will just lend you my expertise and advice. We can go after your husband aggressively or we can just deal with him quietly. Whatever you wish."

Lainey bit her lip. This sounded too good to be true.

"Shall I send the paperwork over?"

She took a deep breath. "Yes, please do." She hoped she wasn't making yet another bumbling mistake. The bottom line was she needed help when it came to Thad and the shop and Mr Bowman sounded like the man who could end this—and quickly.

"You won't regret this, Lainey. We'll talk soon."

* * * *

As promised, by the time Jason entered the shop at quarter to five, Lainey was up to her eyeballs in legalese.

"What's all this?"

Lainey looked up at him. "Um, I think I have a new lawyer?"

"You think you do?"

"Yes, it all happened so fast, I'm a little overwhelmed."

"You took my advice then?"

"Well, not exactly. I didn't actively go shopping for an attorney. He kind of fell into my lap, with some help from a group of lovely ladies that stopped in today. They bought a bunch of merchandise and then, before they left, one of them gave me her son's card and then *he* called *me*."

"Well, that's different," he said slowly.

"I know what you're thinking. That this is stupid on my part. That I shouldn't have agreed to anything. I don't know anything about this man. I'm seriously getting a headache." She rubbed her temples.

Jason picked up the business card that lay on the counter. "Cam Bowman. I've actually heard of him. He's good. He has exclusive clientele. I'm impressed."

Lainey blinked, feeling immeasurably better. "That's not all. Look at this. He found me some silent partners that want to buy into the shop." Lainey turned the document that she'd been reading his way so that he could look it over. "Can you believe that?"

"Partners? If that's all you needed, I could have helped out."

"I wouldn't have let you do that. But thank you for being so sweet."

"So, who are these backers?"

"I don't know. They are only identified in the documents as Divas, V—a division of the West Group. Ever heard of either of them?"

"I've heard of the West Group before. They dabble in all kinds of investments and some real estate, I think."

"So, this is a reputable deal then? I was thinking it sounded too good to be true? Do you think I should go for it? Mr Bowman believes he can have Thad signing off on the house and the shop by the end of next week."

"You don't sound like you're convinced."

"Well, I'm not. It can't possibly be this cut and dry. There has to be a catch somewhere. I just haven't found it yet."

Jason came around the counter and took her in his arms. "And maybe things are just going to go your way for once."

Lainey inhaled his familiar scent. "Twice."

"Twice?"

"I think things turned my way when I walked into your classroom."

"Nope, that's when things started going mine." He smiled sending another round of butterflies through Lainey's stomach.

The bell sounded on the door. "Can you two, seriously, get a room," Henry said, walking into the shop with Jill.

Lainey gave Jason an extra squeeze before she moved from his arms.

"What's all this?" Jill asked of the forms all over the counter.

"Just some legal stuff I was going over," Lainey answered, gathering it up into a pile.

"Something going on?" Jill asked, watching her mother closely.

"Just the same stuff. Nothing to worry about. Did you hear from your dad yet?"

"No. I think I'll call him tonight. I don't even know if he still expects me for the weekend." Jill turned to Henry and by the look she gave him it seemed to Lainey that maybe her daughter didn't want to go visit her dad but stay with her boyfriend instead.

"I'm sure he does. Goodness knows he'd make a federal case out of it if you didn't." Besides, Lainey and Jason had plans to spend the weekend together and she for one was looking forward to spending the nights curled up with him. "What are you two up to?"

"Well," Henry began, "the football team got roped into helping out with the annual school talent show, since Mrs Leadbetter, who was in charge of it, inadvertently fell over one of the football sleds that someone forgot to put away. Broke her freakin' ankle. So Coach Anderson is making us help out and I recruited Jill, since frankly I don't want to do it and it wasn't my fault."

"And I suggested you, Mr Westlake."

"No. I don't think so." Jason declined.

"Why not? This is the first talent show since you became a teacher here. A teacher at our school, with actual talent."

"Yeah, where's your school spirit, Dub?"

"Come on, Jason, for the kids." Lainey grinned encouragingly.

"You're supposed to be on my side."

"I am. I want to hear you sing some more."

"I don't sing in public anymore. I quit, remember?"

"But what better cause to come out of retirement for than your adoring students."

"Okay, I'll do it if you will."

"Me?" Lainey squeaked.

"Yeah, we sounded awesome together in the park. Sign me up. I'll do a duet, Jill, with your mother."

"No, no way. I can't sing in front of a crowd."

"For the kids, Lainey," Jason cajoled.

"Forget it. Forget I said anything."

"Come on, Mom. It'd be awesome." Jill turned excitedly toward her mother.

"This is insane."

"You'll do it?" Jill practically jumped up and down.

Lainey sent Jason a pathetic plea for help. He grinned at her discomfort. She'd backed herself right into that one.

Henry and Jill headed for the door. "Well, that was easier than I thought it would be," Henry said.

"Told ya, piece of cake," Jill responded as the door swung shut.

"This has been the strangest day of my life," Lainey remarked.

"Close up and let's go home, and I'll try to top it."

"Sounds good."

Lainey hurried to close the shop.

* * * *

Jason watched as Lainey pored over the paperwork

spread all over his counter at home. He wished she'd just sign the freakin' papers already. He'd talked to Cam several times during the day. He was Jason's attorney and a family friend. He'd gotten Jason out of quite a few little scrapes while he was living the life of a rock star. Plus, their moms had been best friends since forever.

"I don't see anything wrong, Jason, but I just don't feel right about it. Something seems off. I mean, silent partners? I don't get why they'd want to invest in a sinking ship."

"Well, obviously they don't see it as such. They must see your potential."

"What potential? I've obviously done a fine job, running the place into the ground so far."

"Quit being so hard on yourself. Thad had equal if not more of a hand in bringing the shop to where it is today. He's the one that wants to see it fail. If you leave it up to him, you'll have nothing."

The phone rang. Jason grabbed it.

"Hello?"

"Hello, Jason, your Lainey is lovely. We all loved her. You've done well for yourself for once."

"Thanks, Ma. I think so too."

"Val was brilliant today, the way she pulled out Cam's card. Did Lainey hear from him?"

"Yep."

"I take it by the one word answers you are not alone."

"Ya got that right."

"Okay, I'll talk to you later, Jase."

"Thanks for everything, Mom."

"My pleasure. Bye for now."

"Bye, Mom."

Lainey smiled. "Do you talk to your mom every day?"

"Practically."

"That's so sweet."

"Do you have parents, Lainey? I've never heard you mention them."

"My dad's gone and my mother took off when I was a

baby. I don't even remember her."

"I'm sorry."

She shrugged. "My dad did a good job, considering. When Thad and I found out that I was pregnant, he moved in with my dad and me, you know, after graduation and getting married and all. We didn't stay long, though, before we got our own little apartment."

"Was it just you and your dad? No siblings?"

She shook her head.

"How about you? Are you an only child?"

"Yep, just me. I'm sure my mother thanks the good Lord every day for only one of me."

"I don't know. She seems pretty proud of you."

"Why'd you and Thad only have one?" Jason asked, carefully.

"He was too focused on his career. We didn't really know where we were going to end up either. It's just easier to pick up and transfer one, wherever you get drafted or traded to. I never really missed having another one, though. Jilly kind of broke the mold, you know? She's kinda perfect."

Jason watched the soft look on Lainey's face as she talked about her daughter.

"She is pretty great."

"You don't have to say that. But thank you."

"I mean it. Or I wouldn't say it. So she and Henry look tight again?"

"Mmm. He's a good kid too. I don't mind seeing her with him. That Boyd kid, though—that would be another matter."

Jason laughed. "Are you going to sign those already, so I can jump you before you have to go home?"

"Oh, is that what you're waiting for? I don't need to sign them right away. Jump me now."

He'd rather she sign first but if this was the only way, so be it.

159

Chapter Thirteen

The next day at school, nearing the end of the day, Henry walked into Jason's classroom.

"I think we have a problem, J-Dub."

As Jason looked up at him, Henry slapped a magazine into the middle of his desk.

On the cover was a picture of himself and Lainey, kissing on his front porch.

Gold Digger Sets Sights on Ex Rock God Jase West read the headline.

"Ah, fuck off! Where'd you find this, Henry?"

"They're everywhere and I know that Jill's mom is going grocery shopping tonight, because I have eaten them out of house and home recently."

"Do you know where she shops?"

"Yeah."

"Has Jill seen this?"

"I don't know."

"We've gotta get those magazines out of the store before Lainey sees them. I haven't had a chance to tell her yet."

"I know, why do you think I'm here? But who's to say she doesn't see it somewhere else? Or what if someone mentions it to her?"

Jason shook his head. One problem at a time.

He and Henry rushed to the grocery store and bought up every last magazine.

"This is all well and good, if this is the grocery store Lainey uses? What if she goes somewhere else for a change? Are you sure this is the one?"

Henry got on the phone with Jill and convinced her to go

shopping with her mother after she closed the shop.

"Henry, what are you up to?" Jill asked.

"Okay, Jill, I'm going to level with you. Westlake and I just bought up all the tabloids in the store, don't ask why. You can guess. So you have to make sure your mom goes to that grocery store."

"Oh fer fuck's sake! If my mother is plastered over those fuckin' rags again..."

"She is, and Dub hasn't had time to come clean yet."

"What's the freakin' hold-up?"

"He's gonna tell her this weekend."

There was a long pause. "Okay, but after this, if he doesn't tell her, I will."

"Thanks, Jill. I'll see you later."

Jason held out his hand. "Thanks, Henry."

"No prob, J-Dub. Remember this while grading my next paper."

* * * *

He knew immediately when he walked in that something was off. Lainey looked up from the counter, but the usual warm welcoming smile didn't follow nor did the standard *'Hey, handsome'*.

"Hey, Lainey love," he said.

"Hello, Jase," Lainey remarked.

"What's goin' on?" he asked, carefully.

"You tell me." She turned the laptop his way. His alter ego leered back at him.

Jase closed his eyes and tried to gather himself. *Fuck!* "Lainey. I was going to tell you."

"Why didn't you tell me the first day? Or the second? Or at the coffee shop instead of telling me those women were from the PTA. You had ample opportunity to level with me. Why the secrets?"

"I was afraid that you wouldn't want to see me, because of my past. Because of your experience with Thad. And then there's the press to consider."

"You're right. I wouldn't have wanted to but I'm not sure that I would have been able to resist. You didn't give me that choice. But we'll never know now, will we?"

"Lainey, I'm sorry. I just wanted you to get to know me. The me that I am now. I'm not that guy anymore."

"No. You're not that guy. Or maybe you are. I don't really care. But you are a liar. And I have no use for that kind of person in my life. Please leave."

"Lainey, come on. Hear me out. Please. Can't we just talk about this?"

"There's nothing to say. You should have told me. Instead I had to learn it from yet another person from my past. Who had the time of her life telling me all about you."

"Who?"

"It doesn't matter who. She was some skank back in high school who always had the hots for Thad, but he never gave her the time of day, back then. But she was, apparently, one of the many that he slept with behind my back more recently. In my home, no less. I don't think she knew when she first came in here that I was misinformed, but she took great pleasure in filling in the blanks when she realized I hadn't a clue as to what she was talking about. Poor, pathetic Lainey, she's always the last to know and the first to be lied to."

After gathering up the bank deposit bag, she then closed the laptop and headed for the door. "You know, I should have guessed. The Bugatti all in itself should have tipped me off. I should have gone digging then. Some small time band, huh?" She paused at the door. "Are you leaving, or am I locking you in?"

Jason strode to the door. "Please, can we talk? Will you give me another chance?"

She locked the door then turned to face him. "You know, I probably would have, if you just being Jase West was the only thing. But the underhanded way that you went about 'helping' me with a lawyer, the store and the 'backers' was over the top. The West Group? Really? You couldn't come up with something a little better? And when I asked you if you'd heard of them, you just lied so seamlessly. No thanks. Been there, done that. I'm just glad I didn't sign the papers. You're no better than Thad, *Jase*."

Jason watched as she stalked off down the street toward the bank.

* * * *

Lainey let herself in to her empty house. Jill had gone to visit Thad. This was supposed to be the wonderful weekend alone with Jason. Lainey finally let loose with the tears she'd refused to give in to all day.

Lainey wondered if Jilly knew about her teacher. Of course she must. Everyone else in town seemed to know the truth. The question was why hadn't Jill come clean? Why had she kept Jason's secret? Because she had wanted to protect her mother or had she wanted to sabotage the relationship? And how could she think that about her own daughter? This sucked!

Lainey did what she always did when she was upset. She cleaned.

About every twenty minutes either her cellphone would chime or the house phone would ring. Lainey checked every time just in case it was Jill. But it was Jason.

So when the phone finally rang and it was Jill, Lainey took a minute to get to it. She was up to her elbows in dish suds, so she just hit the speaker button so that she could talk and wash at the same time.

"Hello, Jilly. Made it to Dad's okay?"

"Mom, you have to come." Lainey's heart dropped when she heard the panic in her daughter's voice.

"What's going on, Jill?"

"It's Dad. I told you he wasn't answering my texts. He's in the hospital, Mom."

There was a knock at the door. Lainey turned and was

not surprised to see Jason outside. She hung her head. She didn't want to deal with any of this.

Against her better judgment she opened the door for him.

"Mom, are you still there?" Jill asked.

"Yes, I'm still here." Lainey looked up at Jason stonily. "Where are you?"

"I'm at Dad's right now. I'm waiting for his coach to come and pick me up. He's going to take me to the hospital to see him."

"What's wrong with him?" Lainey had a sneaking suspicion it was drug related and that he was in a rehab center.

Jason closed the door and leaned against the counter, waiting.

"Mom, I think it's bad. The guy who called said something about Post-Concussion Syndrome. It isn't steroids at all. Mama, I think he has brain damage."

She'd never discussed her concerns about steroids with Jill.

Lainey felt dizzy for a moment. It would be much easier to deal with knowing that Thad's sudden change in behavior was drug induced but not this. There was a serious concussion problem going on in several of the major league sports divisions recently. It was all over the news. Hockey and football being hit the worst with this type of serious head injury. Was she to believe that none of this was Thad's fault?

"Mom!"

"Yes, I'm here, Jilly."

"Please. Will you come? I've talked to him. He needs you. He's asking for you." Her daughter sniffed back tears.

"Jill. I can't. I'm sorry. I can't help him. It's not my place anymore."

"What do you mean? It wasn't his fault, Mom! Don't you see? All those awful things he did weren't his fault. He's sick! You have to! Please. For me? If you won't come for him, please, I need you. I don't know what to do."

Lainey looked up at Jason. His expression was impassive.

"Mom!"

"I'll be there first thing in the morning, Jill."

Her daughter dissolved into inconsolable tears after that, then there was a dial tone.

Lainey walked over and hit the speaker button a second time, cutting off the grating noise.

"You're seriously going to go to him?" Jason asked.

"I'm going for my daughter."

"Then I guess this isn't important to you?"

"About as important as it was to you."

"What's changed since this morning? I mean really? What's different? So you know what I used to do for a living, which, in all actuality, I told you. So what? The things that have happened between you and I haven't changed."

"Everything has changed. You lied to me. You can't begin a relationship built on lies. I'll always be waiting and wondering what's next? Just like I did with Thad."

"For one thing, I'm not Thad. But you're running back to Thad anyway. You must love having your heart stomped on."

"Clearly."

"Then I'll get out of your way." He turned for the door. "But let me leave you with one thing that you need to think about while you're off saving Thad. I love you, Lainey, and that's God's honest truth."

He stared at her a good thirty seconds before he walked out.

The horrible truth was she loved him too.

* * * *

Lainey landed at the airport and was greeted by several of Thad's teammates—men who had been to their home in happier times.

"Hi, Kelly," Lainey greeted. "Ben. Doug."

Kelly gave her a quick hug. "I'm really sorry that we have

to see each other again under such dire circumstances, Lainey."

They escorted her to the treatment facility where Thad was being cared for. Jill was there. She embraced Lainey. "Thank you," she sobbed.

Lainey stroked her hair as she turned to face Thad. He was sitting up in the hospital bed. He watched her stoically.

"Come on, Jill, let's go find you something to eat, while your mom and dad talk." Kelly took Jill by the shoulders.

Thad spoke first. "Thanks for coming. I didn't think you would."

"I didn't come for you."

Lips pursed, he nodded slightly.

"I'm sorry, Lainey. For everything that I did."

"Sorry doesn't take it all back, Thad."

"I know."

"And I'm sorry that you are going through what you are, but it doesn't change what you did."

"I know that too."

"Or the things you've done since. I don't believe for one second that you didn't have lucid moments, Thad, where you knew exactly what you were doing."

"You'd be right."

Lainey looked up at the ceiling. What the fuck was she doing here?

"So why am I here, Thad?"

"I needed to apologize, in person. I will regret for the rest of my life what I threw away, Lain." She could almost believe he meant it.

"We had it all. Now, I've got nothing. I've lost you. My career is over. I'll never play ball again. Everything we always wanted. I had it and let it slip right out of my grasp." He covered his face. Lainey sat down in a chair by the bed.

Thad uncovered his tear-streaked face. His obvious pain and sorrow hit Lainey squarely in the chest. "I still love you, Lain. Can you ever forgive me?"

"How can you ask me that?"

"Because I need to know."

She was afraid to answer. She hadn't even spoken to the doctors yet. She had no idea how bad his condition was or what the prognosis might be. What if she said the wrong thing and he hurt himself?

"No. I can't," she answered, quietly.

He gnawed on his lip for a moment. "Jill said you were seeing someone."

"Yes, I was."

"Is it serious?"

"It's too soon to tell." She had no intention of discussing Jason with Thad.

"I never thought you'd see other guys."

"I never thought you'd see other women. But I didn't come here to rehash all that. What do the doctors say?"

"I'm supposed to have an MRI on Monday and a CT scan to check on the severity of the damage. They'll go from there."

She nodded. "We'll go from there."

* * * *

Jason walked into class Monday morning after passing a lousy weekend, surprised to see Jill in her seat.

"Good morning, Jill. How's your dad doing?"

"He's okay, thanks. He has some tests scheduled for today, then I guess we'll know more."

"When did you and your mom get back in?"

"I got in late last night. My mom stayed with my dad," Jill finished, looking down at her desktop and not at him.

Well, that just put everything into perspective and made the knot of dread in his belly ten times worse.

* * * *

Lainey waited in Thad's room while he had his tests and read through the mounds of material the medical staff had left for Thad. The long-term effects of what Thad might be facing were staggering. Post-Concussion Syndrome ran the gamut of symptoms, including headaches, depression, anxiety, irritability, mood swings, vertigo, cognitive problems involving memory, concentration, and thinking, change in behavior, and in some of the more severe cases, the onset of early dementia, and even suicide.

"Hey, you're still here." He seemed happy to see her. "Isn't she great?" Thad said to the nurse pushing his wheelchair. "That's my wife."

"Very nice, Mr Markham."

"Mrs Markham," the nurse acknowledged. Lainey nodded in greeting while helping Thad back into bed. Thad had been playing this game all weekend, using his illness to try to wheedle his way back into her good graces.

"It's Clarkson. Mr Markham and I are one signature shy of divorce."

"Ohh, I'm sorry to hear that," she backtracked.

"Come on, Lain. We've had a great weekend together with Jill, like we were a real family again."

"But we're not. You saw to that."

"The doctor will be in to see you shortly." The nurse left quickly.

Lainey stared out of the window.

"Are you in love with him?" Thad asked.

"With who?"

"The guy you're seeing?"

"I don't know."

"You must be because I don't see the love in your eyes that I used to see when you looked at me."

"Regardless of what I feel for someone else, you still wouldn't see love in my eyes when I look at you, Thad. You successfully squashed that over and over again. The only thing I feel for you now is pity."

"Ouch! I want you back, Lain. I want you by my side while I fight this thing. There's no one but you that can see me through this."

"I'll help you all I can, Thad, but that's all there is to it.

You hurt me. Don't you get it? I hate what you did to us. Those two little teenagers that hated the world but loved each other, do you remember them? They had hopes and dreams and once we achieved them, you left me."

"Then go. I don't need you. Go back to your house and your stupid little store. I'll take it all away from you. Just like you're doing to me."

"What am I taking from you?"

"You're taking you away from me!"

"You're not even making sense."

All of a sudden he batted the container of water from the table in front of him. "Get the fuck out. Go! Go back to your boyfriend, you fuckin' slut!"

"Oh, so I'm the slut," Lainey retorted, picking up the jug. "You go off and do half the town, but I'm the bad guy."

Crossing his arms like a little kid that had just been reprimanded, Thad turned his face away and refused to look at her.

"I love your version of things, Thad." Lainey mopped up some of the liquid with some rough brown paper towelettes from the dispenser. "You don't even make sense."

"I don't have to make sense, my brain is scrambled. Remember?"

"Oh, so is that going to be your new crutch? Blame all your bad behavior on your illness instead of me?"

"Why are you being such a bitch?"

"I'm out. See ya tomorrow. Maybe." Lainey grabbed her purse and made for the door when another object flew across the room and hit the wall just ahead of her.

Lainey turned and leveled her ex with a look. "Good thing you weren't the QB, ya jack wagon!" she yelled childishly before ducking out, then colliding with Thad's doctor.

"Hey, what's all this?" he asked, taking Lainey by the shoulders, worry etched on his kind face.

"Thad is having a little fit."

"I can see that. What set him off?" the physician asked.

"Are you sure about all this, doctor? I mean did you guys

do toxicology tests when you took his blood?"

"That's what I was about to tell him. I have the results back." He gestured for her to go back into the room.

Reluctantly, she did.

"Lainey, I'm sorry," Thad apologized as soon as she re-entered the room. When Lainey didn't respond he turned his attention to the physician. "What's the word, doc?"

"Well, Thad," he began, sitting down. "You are both right. You do have a brain injury. Brain scarring actually."

Thad turned and gave Lainey a smug look.

"From a concussion?" Lainey asked.

"From several, in my opinion. Recurring."

Lainey sighed.

"And your wife is also correct. Thad, you have been using performance enhancing drugs. And by the look of things, for a good long while too."

Lainey bit her tongue lightly so she wouldn't stick it out at him.

"I have not. You're lying!"

The doctor gave him an impatient look. "Blood tests don't lie, Thad. They are not like people."

"So what happens next, doctor?" Lainey asked hoping she could go home soon.

"Well, the good news about the brain scarring is we don't have to operate, but we do want to use a fairly new and very promising procedure called nanotechnology. This treatment not only gets rid of the scar tissue but also encourages brain nerve growth, which can over time repair a good bit of the damage so that you can lead a fairly normal life, Thad."

"What good is that if I can't play ball?" He pouted.

"Then you'll coach, or become a broadcaster, Thad." Lainey tried to get through to him. "Your career was winding down anyway. You're not that young anymore, Thad, face it. You'll just have to find some other way to contribute to the sport you love. With that face and big mouth, I see commentator all over."

When he turned to look at her, Lainey's stomach did a flip. The Thad she had once loved more than anything in the world looked back at her. "And what about us?" he whispered, his eyes filling up.

Cursing herself, Lainey's did too, in response. But she shook her head.

Closing his eyes, he bowed his head and nodded. It was over and they'd both finally accepted it.

"I'm glad to see you're coming to terms with things, Thad," the physician said.

"So when do we start this treatment?" Thad asked.

"That's up to you. You need to commit yourself to a rehab clinic and get yourself cleaned up from the drugs you've been pumping into your body first. When you are rehabilitated, or at least clean, we will begin. I have people waiting right now, if you want to begin right away. Which I strongly suggest you do. Don't fool around with this, Thad. It won't stay like this forever. We have a small window of opportunity to take care of this while you are not permanently impaired. Don't let it close, or we might not be able to help you."

Thad inhaled deeply and looked at Lainey. Shakily, he reached for her. She took his hand. "I should go," he said to her.

She nodded. "You get better for yourself. And Jilly."

"Okay, Doc, I'm ready."

Chapter Fourteen

Lainey stayed with Thad until he was settled in the rehab center then she flew back home. But not before he had signed the divorce papers right in front of her.

When she reached the house it was in darkness. She let herself in and unpacked her things, wondering where Jilly was, until she found the flyer for the talent show.

Sighing, Lainey sat down on a kitchen stool, exhausted. The last thing she wanted to do was go out. But she should be there to support Jill. What she really wanted to do was crawl into a nice hot bubble bath with a glass of wine. And why did that make her think of Jason? Unfortunately, everything made her think of Jason.

Her cellphone buzzed from inside her purse. Reaching lazily for it, she then thumbed the screen.

Hey, Lain. Are you home yet? It was Thad.

Yeah, just got in.
Jilly home?

No. Talent show night.

Are you going?

I should.

I'm sorry, Lain, 4 everything. I love u. But don't let what I did 2 u stop u from being happy. U deserve 2 B.

Lainey had no idea how to respond. And wondered why he was saying these things in a text. Why hadn't he been able to say them to her face? When she could have read sincerity or more underhandedness from his expression.

These were my mistakes. I hope this guy u r seeing is the 1 that can make u happy 4ever.

Lain, u still there?

Yes, Thad, still here. Not sure what 2 say. Wish u could have said this when I was at the hospital.

I'm a coward, Lain. U know that by now. Will he b there 2night? At the show?

Yes.

Go, Lainey. Stop wasting time. I'm beginning 2 realize life's 2 short.

Wow, what kind of rehab center did they put u in? They've worked miracles already.

Ya think? Enough that you'll come back?

There was another pause.

You can't blame a guy for trying. I love u, Lainey. I always will.

Lainey swallowed hard

Get well, Thadeus.

Been a long time since u called me that. :(

I'll always miss my Thadeus. He's gone 4 me. It's like he died. It hurt so much I thought I was going 2 die 2.

I'm so sorry. You'll never know how much. But u didn't, 'cause you're the strong one. U always have been. Go live, Lainey.

A few minutes passed while Lainey sat in a fog of misery and loss. Her phone buzzed one last time.

Goodbye.

She set it down and away from her.
"Goodbye, Thadeus," she whispered.
After dragging herself to the bathroom she then jumped in the shower. But it wasn't Thad's words running through her thoughts anymore. They were Jason's. He was right. What had really changed? Essentially he had revealed the truth about the band, just not the scope. *That's what I gave up to be a teacher*, she remembered he'd said the day of the forgotten hike. She must have been in denial, with the cars and the fancy house. On some level she had to have known.

And there was the declaration that was in her every other thought—'I love you, Lainey, and that's God's honest truth.'

As Lainey drove toward the school, her cellphone chimed again.

Lainey hit the hands free button on the dash. "Hello?"
"Mama, you *are* home."
"Hey, Jilly, I'm almost at the school now…"
"No, wait, listen, you have to hear this."
"Jill? Jill…I…"
"Shut up, Mom and listen, he's singing to you."
What? Who? Jason?

Tuning in, she heard the low tones of an acoustic guitar and that beautiful raspy voice that made her stomach cartwheel.

Straining, she tried to hear the words. She could only decipher every other one, for the noise of the crowd and Jilly holding the phone gave it a muffled, distorted sound. But all the same, the sentiment came through. He was singing Doug Stone's *I Never Knew Love*. Jason knew that it was one of her favorite country love songs.

Lainey covered her mouth, trying to hold back the tears that blinded her.

* * * *

A bunch of students and parent volunteers spent an hour or so cleaning up and stacking chairs.

"Hey, West," one of the other teachers called in passing. "Awesome song. You still got it."

Grinning, he nodded his thanks.

Approaching the main doors, Jason found Henry and Jill waiting there.

"Maybe she just stopped to get something," Henry said, running his hand up and down Jill's back.

"I talked to her on the phone, like, two hours ago and she was in the car and on the way here. What if something happened?"

Jason's stomach tightened.

"Sorry, I didn't mean to overhear, but I did. Are you sure your mom was on the way, Jill? Perhaps she changed her mind and didn't want to be here because of me?"

"No, she wouldn't do that. She wouldn't allow you to stop her from being here to see me. I phoned her when you were singing so she could hear that it was about her. She was on the way. I don't feel right. Something is wrong." Jill stared up at him as if she wanted him to make it all right.

"Why don't you guys stay here and I'll drive from here to your house, Jill. Maybe she got a flat on the way?" Jason said, trying to think up harmless situations that might have detained her mother.

"She would have texted me."

"Maybe her cell battery died," Henry suggested.

"You two give me a call if she shows up here and I'll do the same if I find her between here and home," Jason instructed. "You got my number, right, Henry?"

Henry nodded, giving him a worried look.

Jason was just about to walk out when the principal

approached. "Jill, can I speak to you for a moment?" Jase knew the man enough to know that he had a serious topic to discuss and if that wasn't a tip-off the two state troopers flanking him were.

Jase's stomach knotted more tightly. Jill's frightened gaze widened.

The principal took her into a more private alcove. Jase and Henry followed.

"Miss Markham, these policemen were called to a traffic accident. Your mother was in a fender bender."

"Oh my God! How is she? Can I see her?"

"She's been taken to Memorial. We can take you there now."

"But how is she?" Jill cried, tears rolling down her cheeks.

"She was quite disoriented, Miss, but the prognosis is good. We'll take you to her."

Jill turned, exchanging a look with Henry.

"We'll follow in my car, Jill," Jason reassured.

"Thank you, Mr Westlake."

All the way to the hospital Jason was on edge, cursing the cop leading for not going fast enough.

"Calm down, J-Dub, it sounds like it's not that bad. I'm sure she's fine."

"Yeah, we'll see how you react when someone you love is hurt, kid."

"Is that so?"

"Is what so?" he snapped.

"Someone you love, huh?"

He didn't deny it.

"Yeah, fat lotta good it'll do me," Jase said, wheeling into the hospital parking lot. "Look how I fouled things up. And worst of all is you tried to tell me in the beginning to fess up. Be an adult and just be honest."

* * * *

Jase and Henry remained out in the hall while Jill visited

with Lainey. He so badly wanted to go in and see and feel for himself that she was all right but wondered if it would just upset Lainey more to see him. She had been incredibly hurt and angry the last time he'd attempted to talk to her.

Jill walked out into the hallway and right into Henry's arms.

"How is she?"

"They say she's going to be fine, but they have her so drugged she can't rouse herself enough to talk to me. Her poor nose is broken and already under her eyes is turning black."

"Sounds more like she got beat up," Henry responded.

"The nurse said the airbag went off. She said that's normal and she's lucky that her wrist is only sprained because usually in car accidents when the bag goes off, the driver ends up punching themselves in the face at a high rate of speed, from the force and velocity."

"Huh, I never really thought about that. Seems to me that those things can be worse than some minor accidents."

"Come on, you two, I'll take you home," Jason said to them.

"Don't you want to go in and see her?" Jill looked up at him, her eyes glassy and accusatory.

"You said she's not even coherent, and I'm probably the last person she wants to see right now. She's had enough upset the last few days. Let's go."

As they were going down in the elevator, Henry spoke, "Well, look at it this way, J-Dub — as I see it Jill's dad would be the last person in the world Ms C might want to see, you're just second last."

Tucking his tongue into the corner of his cheek so that he wouldn't lash the kid with it, Jason then took a deep breath.

Jason barely listened to the two teenagers yapping in the back seat. Pulling up outside Lainey's house, Jase popped the car in park. Jill and Henry got out.

"Thanks for the ride home, Mr Westlake."

"Yeah, thanks, J-Dub."

177

Henry slammed the car door.

"Wait, wait, whoa, whoa," Jason said jumping out of the car. "And where do you think you're going, hot shot?"

"I'm going to stay with Jill. She doesn't want to stay here by herself."

Jill blushed to the roots of her hair.

"Yeah, try again. Get in." Jason opened the door for Henry to get back in.

Henry neared Jason and said in hushed tones, "Come on, J-Dub. What the hell are ya doin'?"

Jason grabbed the kid by the collar and sat him forcefully in the passenger's seat then turned to Jill. "Go in the house. Goodnight, Jill," Jason said.

Sitting back in the car, Jason waited until Jill was safely inside before he pulled away.

"That was uncalled for, J-Dub."

"Uncalled for? Do you think I was born yesterday?"

"No, but I know your lifestyle. You can't act like an outraged parent when I've seen the women you've fu—"

"Stop. Right there. That was my life before. And there was no way I was gonna let you stay there alone with her. You two can do that stuff on your own time, but I'll be damned if you're going to do it on my watch. Lainey would kill me. And frankly, I don't want to know."

"Geez, Dub, ya act like we've never do—"

"Shut up, kid! Just shut your damn mouth."

Henry doubled up in hysterics, holding his stomach.

"I'm just shittin' ya, Dub. We haven't yet."

"Jesus, what does 'shut the fuck up' mean to you, kid?" Jason cautioned wearily.

"I'm sorry, I'll be good. But we were just gonna cuddle—"

Jason raised his hand having every intention of backhanding the kid in the chest, but then his teacher senses kicked in and he aborted. *Hands off the students.* Jason knew exactly what cuddling at their age led to, especially when one of the participants was upset.

He pulled up out front of Henry's place and stopped.

"Just get out. Don't say another word."

Henry did as he was told.

"And don't bother going back to the school to get your truck so that you can go back over to Jill's. Go in your own house and go to bed, Henry. You got me?"

Henry nodded, waved and jogged up the path to his house. Again, Jason waited until he went inside before he drove away.

Making a big loop around the block, he then parked just down the street from Lainey and Jill's and waited. It wasn't that long ago that he was a teenage boy too and he wouldn't have listened.

About half an hour later Henry, in his mom's car, drove into Jill's driveway.

Jason watched him from a deckchair in the corner of the darkened porch. Henry rang the bell then cupped his hand and blew into it, checking his breath.

"Ya want a breath mint, kid?"

Henry jumped about a foot in the air, just as the door opened.

"Fuck! You scared the shit out of me!"

Jason moved into the light the open door created. Jill's eyes were huge as she stared at the two of them. She rushed to hold her robe closed and for the second time that night, her face turned bright red.

Jason didn't speak another word, but clamped his hand around the back of Henry's neck and turned him around, resisting the urge to kick him in the ass all the way back to his mommy's car.

After opening the car door, Jason sat him down then closed the door, and promptly followed him home, driving straight on past when Henry parked.

Jason didn't even bother to go to stake out Jill's again. Both kids would think that he was there. Instead he drove back to the hospital.

It was long past visiting hours. He made it all the way up to the floor Lainey was on before he was stopped by one of the nurses.

"Please, I just want to sit with her. So she's not alone. I won't bother her or disturb her."

"Are you her husband?"

Jase hesitated for a moment, ready to go with the lie if it would get him in there.

"No. I'm not. But I hope to be one day. Whoa!" He exhaled, as his own admission sank in. "Wow!"

"Now you look like you need to sit down, sir."

"Then can I go in?"

"No, I'm sorry, we have rules and reg—" Suddenly she narrowed her gaze. Jase knew that look. "Hey, are you Jase West?"

"Yeah, I used to be."

"Well, maybe you can sneak in there for a little bit."

Plastering an obligatory smile on his face, he thanked her.

Jase sat down beside the bed. Lainey did look like she'd been in a fight—eyes puffy and purplish, her entire face seemed somewhat swollen from the deployment of the airbag.

Jase stroked a comforting finger over the back of her bound hand.

Out of the blue, mumbling nonsense, she stirred.

"Jilly...?" she murmured. The anguish in her voice hit him square in the chest.

Jason reached up and stroked her dark hair, crooning softly. "Jilly's fine, my Lainey love. I took her home myself and made sure she was safely in the house. Even put the run on the determined horny little coyote stalking her," he said, the last more to himself.

"Jason?"

"Yeah, babe, I'm here."

It seemed to calm her. He took some solace in that at least. She didn't curse him out or demand that he leave her room and she hadn't called for Thad.

"Ahh, Lainey, you don't know how scared I was when I found out you were hurt. You mean so much to me. I don't want to waste any more time. I know we just met and that you hate what I did, but I want to be with you." Discouraged, he shook his head.

"You have to forgive me. Can you believe I didn't take my own advice? People who don't learn their history are doomed to repeat it and I made the same damn mistakes. I've no idea where to start to make it up to you, but I'm going to show you that you can trust me." He ran his hand over his mouth. "If I could go back, you'd never shed a tear. I'd take things slow, just like I promised. I'm not Jase West anymore. I'm Jason Westlake and I love you. I won't give up, my Lainey love, so be prepared. I'm gonna fight like hell to make you see that you're the one for me. We were meant to be."

Laying his head down on his arms, he kept a light hold on Lainey.

"I love you too, Jase," she mumbled.

To Jason, there were no sweeter words ever spoken.

* * * *

Lainey woke groggily, slowly taking inventory of all her aches and pains. Moving stiffly, she realized she wasn't alone. She tried desperately to open her eyes, but found the action difficult. When she'd accomplished that small task, she looked down to find Jason's dark head tucked into her side.

Too weak and defeated to cry, she moved her fingers on the side of his face and he roused.

"Lainey? How are you?" Even half asleep, she could see the concern on his handsome face. She didn't even want to know how bad she looked.

"I'm doing just fine. Don't worry about me."

"Easy for you to say."

"Were you writing a new song earlier?" she mumbled.

"No, why?"

"I thought I heard the makings of a very sweet love song."

"I was merely pouring out my heart."

"Well, I think you'd better write that one down. I think it's a hit."

"None of that means anything to me, if you're not in my life."

The sincerity in his eyes might not have been enough a few days before, but it was now. Thad was right. Life was too short. And she would not suffer regrets where Jason Westlake was concerned. She couldn't allow him to get away and spend the rest of her life wondering.

"Perhaps someday you might sing it, at, say...a wedding?"

His dark gaze darted.

"Are you saying what I think you are?"

Lainey tried to smile through stiff, swollen lips.

"Did you just ask me to marry you?" he asked, looking relieved and smug all at the same time. His grin widened. "Well, I just don't know what to say, Lainey. This is so sudden. I wasn't expecting—"

"Jason!"

He chuckled and it warmed her heart even more.

"Yes, I could definitely sing that at a wedding."

"Oh? Do you know someone getting married?" Lainey asked innocently.

"Oh, you are a witch."

"I've been called worse. Just recently."

"I'm sure I don't want to know."

He kissed her forehead.

"I was so scared."

"I know, I heard you. But I'm going to be all right and we are too."

"And what about Thad?"

"Thad's going to be fine and hopefully be around a good long time for Jilly."

"Just like I'll be around for our own kids?"

Lainey paused. "Our kids?" she asked slowly.

"Let's not have that conversation right now."

"Good choice." Lainey moved over making room. Jason

hopped into bed, gathered her close and rocked her gently.

Epilogue

Jase and Lainey sat up in bed reading the Sunday paper.

"Hey, Ma, have you seen the cover of People?" Jill called from the room she'd picked out as her own in Jason's house. At least for the limited amount of time she would stay in it before she started college.

"No, why?"

"They've got a great photo of your and my new daddy's engagement announcement."

Lainey and Jase shared a conspiratorial smile.

"When do you think the press will find out that we're already married?" Lainey asked her new husband.

"Oh, I'm guessing any time now." Jase was incredibly proud of himself for pulling off the wedding and the honeymoon without the paparazzi discovering any of the details. No cameras, no helicopters, no event-crashers. It had been a small intimate affair and the best day of his life.

"Hey, Jase?" Jill bellowed.

"Yes, my lovely new daughter," he called back, tongue in cheek.

"Did you see Jase West's Rock Me Gently hit Number One in the Billboard charts?"

"It did? That's awesome."

"Now the press is clamoring for a Jase West comeback."

"Well, they're shit outta luck. Jase West has officially retired."

"What about Jason Westlake?" Lainey asked, watching him steadily.

"Jason Westlake is a husband, a father, a teacher, and a songwriter. In that order. And if I do any more recording, it will be with my lovely wife."

Leaning over, he then kissed her on the lips.

"When are we going to tell Jilly about the other little duet we got goin' on?" Jason placed his hand possessively over her tiny swelling tummy.

Lainey opened her mouth to speak when Jill stuck her head in their room.

"Do you two really think that I'm sooo naive that I don't know there's a little rock star in the oven? Really? Give me some freakin' credit here. Gawd! Does it say paps on my forehead?" She lifted up her bangs and stared closely into the mirror. "No, it clearly does not."

"Your new daughter is a smart-ass," Lainey remarked.

"Yeah, she takes after her mother. We can only hope this one takes after me."

Lainey tossed a newspaper at him. He used it as a good excuse to tackle her and wrestle her onto her back and kiss her senseless.

"Oh, you two, will you get a room...? Oh wait, I guess this is your room. Carry on!"

Jill backed out quietly, closing the door.

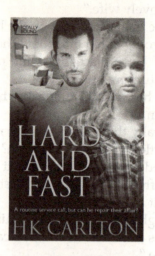

Hard and Fast

Excerpt

Chapter One

Josslynn Rossdale stood in line at the bank. Another scorching day with the humidity so high that one perspired just standing still. Most of the other customers appeared to be melting, each with that fine layer of sheen and flushed complexion. In a lightweight cotton blouse, beige short shorts and sandals, Joss attempted to beat the heat.

"Next," the first vacant teller drawled.

Joss stepped forward.

"Hey, Joss, how are you?" She'd been in the savings and loan so often lately that the employees knew her by name.

"Good, Tracey, and you?"

"It's so much better in here now that they've got the air conditioning back up and running."

Joss noted the serviceman in the standard blue work shirt, placing his tools back into his box. "Mmm, should suggest him for my building. AC's on the fritz at my apartment too. I put in a call to the building manager but I'm still waiting."

The repairman was tall, with short dark hair and nice broad shoulders. Snug, navy workpants showcased his well-toned glutes. As if he knew that he was being scrutinised he turned and zeroed right in on Joss. He had the most piercing blue eyes. *Too cute, and too young.* He couldn't be more than twenty-five, she guessed. Somewhat used to a certain amount of healthy male attention herself, she smiled, totally aware that he was checking her out too. He grinned in return and the action brought out a charming dimple in his left cheek. He sported a fine layer of stubble as if he hadn't had time to shave that morning. Joss liked it. It gave him a rugged appearance. Yes, he was a very attractive guy.

"What can I help you with, Joss?" Tracey snagged Joss' attention back. "He's really freakin' hawt, right?" Tracey said under her breath, just as the young workman set down his toolbox on the countertop next to her workspace.

"Actually, I was hoping to catch Tom," Joss answered. "I'm not sure if he's in, but he said he'd leave some paperwork for me at the customer service wicket. But your man Tech-Co here is using it to store his tools at the moment." Joss read the company name off the guy's shirt.

"Sorry, I didn't mean to interrupt. I just need a signature and then I can get out of the way." He said this to Tracey but kept his gaze trained on Joss, grinning, the corner of his mouth curling adorably.

"I'll get the manager. I'm not taking responsibility for anything," Tracey scoffed, leaving her post.

"Hi," Tall, Dark and Handsome said simply. He had a pleasant, deep baritone voice.

"Hi," she responded.

"It's another hot one, huh?"

"Sweltering," Joss agreed.

He peered directly into her eyes. She liked it but it was also a little disarming.

"I hear it's supposed to be this way all weekend," he added.

"That's what I hear."

His lips were nicely shaped, the bottom one nice and full.

"I guess I shouldn't complain. It keeps me busy."

"I imagine."

On even closer examination, under that dark and grainy stubble was a slight cleft. Joss was a sucker for a man with a dent in his chin.

"Here we go. The manager is on the way," Tracey said to the repairman. "And, Joss, here's the portfolio Tom put together for you to go over."

"Thanks, Tracey. I'll probably see you again in the next week then."

"Yep, see ya then. Next!"

Joss glanced back at TD&H. "Have a good day then," she said lamely.

"Yeah, you too." He nodded as the manager joined him.

Joss began to walk out when one of the other financial managers stopped her to make sure she'd been waited on. She assured him that she had, thanked him kindly then continued to the exit, arriving as the rugged repairman did. It just so happened his hands were full—toolbox in one and a ladder in the other. Joss held the first door open for him.

"Well, thank you," he said with a wide smile. He had excellent teeth too.

Joss rushed ahead and opened the second door.

"Thanks again." He squinted up at the sky. "Whoa, it is hot out here. Being in there, in the cool, makes you forget for a while."

"I know. It's nasty, isn't it?" Joss let the door swing closed and she turned in the direction of her car.

"Take care," he said then continued on his way.

For shits, Joss peeked over her shoulder, and to her delight, he was doing the same thing. How sad had her life become that she was now thrilled by such a little thing?

More books from HK Carlton

Behind his beauty hides a secret.

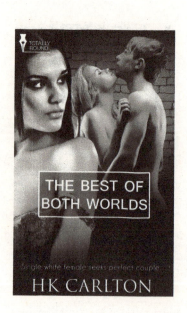

Single white female seeks perfect couple…

About the Author

HK Carlton

H-K lives in Canada with her hard-working hubby. She has two very handsome grown sons and a beautiful teenage daughter. She has been an avid reader all her life. Her first love is historical romance so it would come as no surprise that her favourite book of all time is Jane Eyre. But she'll read almost anything that captures her attention and imagination. She loves nothing more than to find a good book that she can't put down. She is a hopeless romantic and prefers happy endings.

HK Carlton loves to hear from readers. You can find contact information, website details and an author profile page at https://www.totallybound.com/